WILD LIGHT

WEST COUNTRY TRILOGY
BOOK THREE

WILD LIGHT

WEST COUNTRY TRILOGY
BOOK THREE

JOHANNA CRAVEN

CONTENTS

DREAMING……………………………………………11

ENEMIES………………………………………....13

THE GOOD AND DECENT MAN………………….23

INCANTATIONS……………………………….....31

RUINS……………………………………………38

THE DOMAIN OF DESPERATE MEN…………….46

THE GIRL WITH LIGHT FINGERS…...........……..65

OLD SILENCE……………………………….....71

REPRIEVE……………………………………..87

LOCKED DOORS…………………………..97

THE DEMONS OF BRIDLES LANE…………….101

UNGODLY THINGS………………………………106

A BLACK SHIP……………………………………115

LOYALTIES…………………………………122

BRUTAL MEN……………………………………132

PRECIOUS INFORMATION………………….....139

THE HEALING WELL……………………………143

CONFESSION……………………………………150

GHOSTS IN SHADOWS…………………………156

HIDING PLACES…………………………………161

A THING OF RETRIBUTION………………….....170

CLIFFTOPS……………………………………...175

BURNING LIGHT…………………………………181

REVENUE MEN…………………………………...191

SPLINTERING……………………………………196

DEBTS……………………………………………200

TRUTHS AND LIES……………………………207

FAITHFUL MEN……………………………………212

TRUST…………………………………………...217

WILD………………………………………………224

BLACK MAGIC…………………………………232

THE ESCAPING SOUL...244
SILENCE...254
TOMORROW..258

HISTORICAL NOTE ON THE WEST COUNTRY
TRILOGY..265

ABOUT THE AUTHOR...269

DREAMING

Her fevered dreams are like this: drowned sailors and haunted hills and the shadows of giants screeching at the sky. She is back in the cave, hearing the sea behind her, feeling herself fall.

Scarlett cries out. The sound sends the sea and the cave away, but the world is still as dark as a barrow. She tries to sit. Her head is thundering. The blackness makes everything unsteady.

Footsteps come towards her.

"Scarlett?" It is Flora's voice. She feels hands on her shoulders, easing her downwards. "Stay still."

"Where am I?" Scarlett's breath is loud in her ears. Fast. Frantic. She gulps down air. Feels as though she is drowning.

"You're at the inn," says Flora.

Pain sears Scarlett's head as she moves on the pillow. She remembers it distantly; the footsteps in the sand behind her, the sudden, splintering blow to the back of her skull. "Light the lamp," she coughs. "I can't see."

Sounds break through the desperate rattle of her breath. Birds. Hooves in the street. The muffled sigh of the sea. There is a strange warmth on her cheek that must be fire or sun.

She reaches into the dark. "Light the lamp," she says desperately. "Please. Light the lamp at once."

She feels Flora's hands at the tops of her arms.

"Lie down, Scarlett," she is saying. "Lie down." Somehow she sounds both close and far away.

"Light the lamp," Scarlett says again. But her voice is faint and fading. There is pain in her head and an invisible sun on her cheek. She lets herself sink back into the bed, lets Flora smooth the blankets she has entangled in her terror. And the fear that engulfs her is hot and sharp as she blinks and blinks again and still she sees nothing.

ENEMIES

The blood is like ink in the sand. Isaac can't pull his gaze from it.

His sister's blood? His wife's?

His infant daughter's?

He and Caroline have spent hours tearing through Polperro, searching for their missing children. Racing from the pilchard palace to shops and houses, questioning, hunting for someone with knowledge. Anyone who might have heard the cry of a child, or seen a man entering the cave with a weapon in his hand.

Their fruitless search has brought them back to this thread of beach inside the cliff where blood is staining the sand.

"Tell me what you saw," Isaac says, for at least the third time.

Caroline's answer is the same. After Reuben's men had stormed their cottage, she had raced to Polperro, desperate to escape the village. Had sheltered in the cave on the beach while Will Francis rowed out to fetch Isaac from the lugger.

But she had not been hidden. She had seen shadows come towards the cave. Heard footsteps in the water. One person. Perhaps more. She had pushed Mary into Gabriel's arms. Watched as her children disappeared into the narrow passage at the back of the cave.

She had been struck from behind, her eyes locked with Mary's. Had awoken to find Scarlett unconscious on the sand beside her and the children gone.

Behind her tears, Caroline's eyes are critical. Isaac had left them. Left his family in the cave to go for Flora.

He had truly believed her in danger, he reminds himself. Had truly believed the smugglers' banker would kill her for helping to deceive Reuben. But it does nothing to ease his guilt.

"Perhaps Gabriel ran," he says, desperately trying to make himself believe it. "Perhaps they're hiding somewhere." But he knows his crimes have left him surrounded by enemies. Knows it far more likely his children have been taken. He folds his hands behind his head. "The revenue men have eyes all over this village. Perhaps they saw something. We ought to ask at Customs House."

Caroline gnaws her thumbnail. "The revenue men have their eyes on you. If we tell them about the children they'll start digging into our life. Is that what you want?"

Isaac paces the thin curve of the beach, letting the sea wash over his boots. "I don't care what they find. I just care about getting the children back."

"*I* care what they find." Caroline's voice rattles. "I can't lose you too."

Isaac opens his mouth to speak. Says nothing. He doesn't deserve her loyalty.

"Bring the revenue men into this and you'll put Scarlett in danger," she reminds him. "And Flora." Her voice is clipped.

Caroline is right, of course. The revenue men are waiting for an excuse to pry, to dig. And if Isaac falls he will take half the village down with him. There can be no going to the authorities. This is theirs to carry alone.

Caroline turns to look back at the village. Clouds lie on top of the hills, drawing the light from the day. "We ought to go to Reuben again," she says.

Charles Reuben's had been the first door they had pounded on. Had been told by his housekeeper the man was unavailable. A sign of his guilt, surely.

Isaac gives Caroline's shoulders a gentle squeeze. "I'll go to Reuben. You go home. Rest. You've been hurt."

She shrugs out of his grasp. "How could I rest? I need to keep looking. There are people in this village we've not spoken to."

After a moment, Isaac says: "Be careful. Please."

She nods faintly. Turns to leave.

"Caroline. Wait." He reaches into the water, wetting the cuff of his shirt. He wipes gently at the line of dried blood streaking the side of her face. He leaves his fingers against her cheek for a moment. It makes his chest ache.

Caroline pushes past him and makes her way into the village.

Isaac strides up the path towards Reuben's mansion. And for the first time, he feels it. That wild rage that takes hold of his sister, that had taken hold of his father. That rage in their blood. He feels it writhe inside him, trying to force its way out. It quickens his heart and makes his skin burn, despite the icy sting of the wind.

He must keep calm. If Reuben has the children he must bend to his requests. This is not a time to lose control.

He draws in a long, slow breath, trying to still his rage. And he understands, fleetingly, what it is like to be Scarlett. Feels what it is like to have that anger batter around inside. A faint glimpse inside the head of the fiery, willful sister he had scooped from the rim of the sea.

He had found her in the cave, blood running from the back of her head and turning the water pink.

Dead, he had thought. Their last words to each other ones of bitterness and anger.

But no, a faint pulse. Breath tickling the back of his hand.

Isaac pulled her from the water's edge as the tide surged towards her. Her blood vanished into the tarred black sleeve of his coat.

For a moment, he stood motionless, frozen with the unbearable horror of it.

Scarlett, Gabriel, Mary. The dried blood at the side of Caroline's head. He felt the weight of his sister in his arms, felt the weight of the situation pressing down on him. It was suddenly hard to breathe.

"Isaac," Caroline said in a half voice. It drew him out of his daze.

He looked up. There were people at the harbour. Two women rolling a barrel past the door of the pilchard palace. Will Francis roping the dory to the quay. Isaac carried Scarlett towards him. Will leapt from the boat at the sight of them.

"Take her to Flora."

Isaac knows nothing of what has happened to his sister.

How long has it been since he had watched Will carry her over the cliffs? Three hours? Four? Perhaps more.

He has no thought of whether Scarlett is still alive.

He pounds on Reuben's door, throwing his rage into the brass knocker until he feels it will break with the force of it. But when the maid answers, he finds himself eerily calm. Anger will not pull answers from Reuben. Anger will not help him find his children.

He follows the maid into the parlour and waits for Reuben to appear. He paces, hands folded behind his head. His boots click rhythmically on the polished boards. Distant sounds come from within the house; laughter and the clink of knives against plates. The smell of roasting meat turns his stomach.

Charles Reuben enters the parlour, his lips pressed into thin white line. He is dressed in a gold-threaded waistcoat and pristine tailed white wig. He looks at Isaac as though he were a stray dog who had weaselled its way through the door. "Bold of you to come to me," he says. "Are you here to make your apologies? I trust you've realised what will happen if you betray me again."

"Where are they?" Isaac asks evenly.

Reuben folds his arms across his thick middle. "Where are who?"

Isaac feels a line of sweat run down his back at the effort of remaining calm. "Let's not play games."

"I've guests, Mr Bailey. And you are taking up my valuable time. Believe me, I'm in no mood to play games either."

Isaac clenches his teeth. "Someone has taken my children," he says. "And attacked my wife and sister."

Reuben hums. "It seems your deceitfulness has bought you a number of enemies."

Isaac lifts a glass ashtray from the side table. He needs something in his hands, something to tense his fingers around, something to channel this anxiety into.

"I don't have your children," says Reuben.

No, this is too easy. He will not just turn away at Reuben's word. Isaac's fingers tighten around the ashtray. "You expect me to believe you had no part in this?"

Reuben meets his eyes. "I am a good and decent man, Mr Bailey. I don't lie. You know that. I've never been anything but honest with you."

"You had your men come after my family this morning," says Isaac. "And you sent the banker after me and my seven-year-old sister. Had him hold a gun to our heads."

"Because you were trying to avoid paying debts that are legally and rightfully yours."

Isaac draws in a long breath, trying to slow his heart. "I will stay here," he hisses. "I will stay here and run goods for you for the rest of my life. Just let my children go."

"Yes," Reuben says evenly. "You will stay here and run goods for me until every penny of your father's debt is paid off, because that is what a decent man would do." He runs a finger over the top of an armchair. "But I do not have your children."

Isaac hurls the ashtray. It shatters on the floorboards with a satisfying crash. Glittering shards escape across the room and settle beneath the clavichord.

A tiny smile appears in the corner of Reuben's lips. "You have much of your father in you, Mr Bailey. It's taken me some time to see it."

Caroline catches a glimpse of herself in the window of the Ship Inn. Her eyes are underlined with shadow, her hair tangled down her back. Blood stains the edges of her cap. She pulls it from her head and bundles it into her fist. Rakes her fingers through her knotted hair.

Looking like a madwoman will not help her cause.

She rattles the door of the tavern. Locked. Inside, she sees the innkeeper wiping a cloth along the bar. She raps loudly on the window. The innkeeper shoos her away.

"We're closed," he calls, his voice muffled through the glass.

Caroline knocks again, louder.

Finally, the man pulls the door open a crack. "What do you want?"

"I need to speak with you," she says breathlessly. "Please. It's very important."

With a sigh, the innkeeper steps back, letting her inside.

The tavern is quiet. Dust motes dance in a shaft of sun that highlights the deep scratches on the tabletops. The innkeeper looks expectantly at Caroline.

"Did you have a man take a room here last night?" she asks, pinning him with eyes that tell him she wants answers, not questions. If Asher Hales is to be believed, Jacob Bailey had asked for a room here after he had confronted her on the beach yesterday. But then, Asher Hales is not a man to be believed. She cannot pretend to be surprised when the innkeeper says:

"No ma'am. Just our regular lodgers in last night."

Caroline goes to the Three Pilchards. There is a sickening symmetry to it. She steps through the door with her bloodied cap in her hand, more lost and undone than she had been that night sixteen years ago when she had walked into this place and told Jacob to abandon his family. And here she stands, looking for the man again.

She approaches the bar slowly. Clears her throat. "I'm searching for a man who is staying at your inn."

The innkeeper lifts a leather-bound ledger from beneath the counter. "Name?"

Caroline watches him flick through the pages. "He'll not have given you his real name. But he would have come to you last night."

"I weren't working here last night. My brother was. Can't help you without a name."

She reaches over the counter and plants a hand in the middle of the book to stop him closing it. "Someone has taken my children. And this man may know something." She smacks her palm against the pages, making the innkeeper start. "Last night. Who was here?"

He narrows his eyes, then after a moment, looks back at the ledger. "Room two," he tells her finally. "A man come in yesterday afternoon."

Caroline feels a sudden thumping behind her eyes. She manages a nod of thanks.

She makes her way upstairs on shaky legs and pounds on the door of room two. Nothing but silence. She can't pretend to be surprised.

Each minute that passes, she is more and more certain that Jacob is the one who has taken her children. He will want her to suffer as he had suffered. Will want her scared, desperate, ready to spill her secrets. Of course he is not here waiting for her.

She presses her eye to the keyhole. Sees nothing but rumpled bed clothes and a bare, scratched table. She makes her way down the hall, peering through the keyholes into the other rooms. More rumpled bedclothes. More empty tables. A woollen bonnet in one room. A riding officer's jacket in another.

Nothing to hint at the whereabouts of Jacob and her children. Nothing to suggest that the world might not be carrying on as though nothing at all has happened.

She gnaws on her thumbnail until the skin around it is red and raw. She sinks to the floor in the hallway outside Jacob's empty room and brings her knees to her chest.

Jacob wants her to leave Talland. Leave Isaac. He had made threats against Mary. But surely he knows she will not leave without knowing her children are safe?

She will do anything to save them. Will tell Isaac her every secret if it will see Mary and Gabriel safely returned. That's what Jacob wants isn't it? For her to look into her husband's eyes and tell him of how she had torn apart his family? She knows the only way Isaac will believe such things are if they come from her own mouth.

But she needs Jacob's word. Her son and daughter in exchange for her secrets. She will not destroy her marriage if it will not give her back her children.

She lets her eyes close. In her mind's eye she sees Gabriel creeping into the passage at the back of the cave. Sees Jacob leaning over Mary's basket. Sees Isaac with his lips against Flora's.

She opens her eyes. Blinks hard and swallows the sickness in her throat.

The stairs creak and she leaps to her feet, pressing a hand to the wall as dizziness cows her.

"You're still here?" the innkeeper demands. "You can't just wait around on the floor all day. What will my customers think?"

"Customers," Caroline snaps. "You've got no customers. I've not seen a soul."

The innkeeper jabs a finger towards the staircase and she makes her way out of the inn, the ache in her chest intensifying.

Jacob Bailey, she realises sickly, will be found when he wants to be.

THE GOOD AND DECENT MAN

Scarlett hears footsteps coming closer. Her fingers tighten around the edge of the blankets. How terrifying the sound is now she cannot see who is approaching.

"Who's there?"

"It's me, Scarlett."

Tears spill suddenly down her cheeks. She is so glad to hear Isaac's voice.

The bed moves beneath his weight. His arms slide around her, pulling her close. She feels his hair tickle her nose, feels his bristly chin against her ear. He smells of salt and sweat and ash soap.

The muscles in his arms are tense. She can tell something is very wrong.

The memories swing at her suddenly.

Isaac had been planning to escape. Had made a run to Guernsey without Reuben's knowledge. Bought liquor from an agent of his own.

Scarlett remembers trying to hide the contraband from

Reuben. Remembers racing home to find the cottage empty. Remembers Asher Hales sending her to the beach in Polperro.

They're in the cave, he had told her. *Your family. I saw them.*

She had found Caroline lying motionless on the sand, blood running from the side of her head.

"Caroline," she says suddenly. "Is she—"

"She's all right. You're not to worry yourself over her."

"Then what?"

There is silence for a moment. Finally, Isaac says:

"Gabriel and Mary are missing. They've been taken by whoever attacked you."

Scarlett feels suddenly hot and sick. The pain in her head intensifies. She opens her mouth to speak, but what is there to say? Her stomach knots.

"Do you remember seeing anything?" Isaac asks. "Before…" His hands are tight around her wrists, steadying her or himself, Scarlett is unsure.

And she is back in that cave, seeing the water sweep through shafts of white light. Watching blood run over Caroline's hair, watching Gabriel's arms reach towards her in fear. These cannot be the last things her eyes ever see.

Movement. Yes, there had been movement behind her. She had seen it fleetingly on the edge of her vision.

"They struck me from behind," she says. "I didn't turn in time to see who it was. I'm sorry."

How useless her words are.

"Reuben found your ankers in the tunnel," she tells Isaac. "Was he the reason Caroline was hiding in the cave? Do you think he took the children to stop you from leaving?"

"Scarlett, I don't want you involved. You need to rest. I only asked in case there was anything you remembered."

"Don't keep things from me," she says, pulling herself into sitting. "Not now. I couldn't bear it."

Isaac doesn't speak at once. "I confronted Reuben," he says finally. "He claims to know nothing."

"He's lying."

"Perhaps."

"I saw the look in his eyes when he found those ankers," says Scarlett. "He was angry enough for this. And he's always been willing to do anything to stop us from leaving."

She had been seven years old the night they had tried to escape. She remembers walking across the beach with Isaac, picking their way in moonlight towards the path on the cliff. Remembers the glow of the lantern spilling over the beach, illuminating the gun in the banker's hand.

Run, Isaac had told her, his big hand clasping hers. But even as a child she had known. Had known Reuben's men would not hesitate to shoot.

Nor would they hesitate to take Gabriel and Mary. Would see it a fitting punishment for Isaac's betrayal.

"I'm sorry," she says suddenly. "For all I said. For the things I accused you of. I'm so sorry. I—"

Isaac brushes the hair from her eyes, the way he used to do when she was a child. "It doesn't matter," he says. "None of it matters. Not anymore."

Finally, Scarlett agrees to rest. Isaac watches as she curls up on her side, moving carefully on the pillow to avoid the swelling at the back of her head.

She closes her eyes. Isaac is glad of it. Her drifting,

JOHANNA CRAVEN

unfocused gaze has made knots of his stomach. Scarlett had been his to protect. Gabriel and Mary, his to protect. And look how he has failed them.

He makes his way into the hallway, closing the door gently behind him.

Where is Flora? He knows it best, of course, that he disappear out of the inn without speaking with her. But he doesn't want that. Doesn't want to disappear. Doesn't want her to disappear.

He hears the clatter of glasses in the bar. She has taken everything from the shelves and is polishing the wood with beeswax. She wears an apron over faded, rose-coloured skirts, her blonde hair in a messy knot at her neck.

She squeezes the polishing rag between her fingers. At once there is everything and nothing to say.

"Any word?" she asks.

Isaac shakes his head. "Reuben denies everything." His eyes drift to the bare shelves.

Flora follows his gaze. "It's a trivial thing to do, I know. But I couldn't bear to keep still."

Isaac gives her a small smile. He remembers this about her. In the weeks after her husband had died, he had called on her each day. Would find her cleaning windows or blacking the hearths, or hemming and re-hemming every item of clothing her daughter owned.

I couldn't bear to keep still, she'd told him.

"Are you sure Scarlett is all right here?" he asks.

"Of course. She'll stay as long as she needs."

"Do you think this will be permanent?" His voice comes out husky.

Flora sighs, tugging at the rag. "I've no way of knowing. I'm sorry." She comes out from behind the bar and presses a gentle hand to his elbow. In spite of himself, Isaac feels his insides heat. His desire for her is still there, poorly hidden, simmering inches beneath the surface. He tries to will it away.

"This isn't your fault," she says. "None of it is your fault."

He doesn't reply. How can he stop believing this his fault? Had he not run back to Talland for Flora, none of it would ever have happened.

"I'd best go," he says.

Flora nods, pulling her hand away. "You'll be in my prayers. You and the children."

When Isaac returns to the cottage, the windows are dark. Caroline has not returned.

He had wanted her to be home. Had wanted to tend to her a little before he went back out to search. Make a fire for her to rest in front of. Tea to warm her.

A fire and tea, of course, will not make up for his betrayal. But perhaps they might begin to show her how deeply he still cares.

He steps inside. Immediately, the silence hits him. An awful, thick stillness without the chattering of a baby or a little boy's footsteps or Scarlett's sassy asides.

How desperately he had wanted to leave this life behind. But now, to sit around the kitchen table with his family, planning the next run to Guernsey feels like the greatest of unreachable joys.

He lights a lamp and his breath leaves him. At his feet lies their upturned travelling chest. Pots and pans are on their sides by the hearth. Clothes have been flung across the cottage. A shirt has found its way into the fire grate, underskirts lying beneath the table. Had Reuben's men done this?

Behind the scattered clothes and pots, the house is spotless.

The shelves are bare and dusted, the grate empty of ash, the wash stand polished and dried. Caroline had readied the house for their escape. Exactly what had happened to make her run?

I'm a good and decent man, Reuben had told him.

Lies, every word. There is no decency to Charles Reuben. No goodness. Are Gabriel and Mary hidden somewhere in the passages of that great sprawling mansion? Had they heard the laughter around Reuben's dinner table that afternoon? Had they been close enough to hear their father's voice?

For all Reuben's denial, Isaac can't get past the thought that he and his men are responsible for the kidnapping. Punishment for his daring to double cross him, as his father had done so many years ago.

How far would Reuben go? Surely his business brain would not seek to kill Isaac's children. They are the ones who will carry the debt when he dies. The thought is both sickening and faintly comforting.

He gathers the clothes from the floor and throws them back in the wardrobe. Closes the door to the empty nursery so his wife might be saved from looking inside. He sets the pots back on the shelf. The sight of them reminds him that neither he or Caroline have eaten all day. He has no appetite, but he knows a little supper will do them both good.

He takes the lamp to the garden and pulls a few potatoes from the damp earth. Carries them inside and lights the fire.

The door creaks open. Caroline collapses into a chair at the kitchen table. "What did Reuben say?"

"He denies everything. Claims himself a good and decent man."

She stares into the flames, a curtain of dark hair falling over one eye. "And you've only just returned?"

Isaac wipes his muddy hands on his breeches. "I went to

see Scarlett."

"You went to the inn." Her voice is cold.

"To see my sister."

For a moment, Caroline doesn't speak. "How is she?" she asks finally.

Isaac feels a heaviness in his stomach. He can't bear to speak the words. *Blow to the head. Blinded.*

"Alive," he manages. "Scarlett is alive."

Caroline pulls her shawl around her shoulders, edging her chair closer to the fire. She looks up at Isaac with watery eyes. "What now?" she asks. "How are we supposed to just carry on?"

He crouches beside her, covering her hand with his. She is stiff, unresponsive.

He has no answer for her. Has no thought of how to make this better. And so he says: "I'm sorry."

Caroline pulls her hand out from beneath his.

"I know it'll not fix anything. And I know it won't help us find the children. But I truly believed she was in danger. That's the only reason I went back."

Caroline is silent for a long time. "A good wife ought to turn her back on such things," she says finally.

Isaac closes his eyes. Guilt tightens his insides. He goes to the table for the potatoes.

"Don't bother," says Caroline. "I couldn't eat."

No. Nor could he.

"Try to sleep," he tells her huskily. "You need it." He sees the fire reflected in her glistening eyes.

"How could I sleep?"

"You need to try. I'll go back out. Look for the banker. He may know something."

Caroline shakes her head.

Isaac presses a firm hand to her shoulder. "Go and rest. I wish it. As your husband."

She snorts. "You wish it," she repeats coldly. "As my husband." The chair squeals noisily as she stands. She disappears into the bedroom without another word.

INCANTATIONS

Scarlett wakes and the images that had lit up her dreams are gone. This is the second time she has woken to darkness and the shock of it is still raw. She touches the swelling at the back of her head. There is something vaguely steadying about the pain. It anchors her to the world she cannot see.

The darkness is deep and wide, littered with pricks of phantom light, too tiny, too imperceptible to be anything but her eyes struggling to make sense of their new futility. She forces herself to breathe slow and deep. She cannot let herself feel anger at whoever had done this to her. The dark has always been able to send her anger away, but how will it be now dark is all she has? If the Wild traps her here, there may be no way of ever getting out.

Inhale. She smells the enchanting scent of drying herbs. Smells the evidence of that healing woman's life Flora had sworn would not be hers.

Scarlett runs a hand over the wall beside the bed, feeling stone worn smooth. She needs to place herself in this world, in this room that had been the village charmer's. She feels the rough grain of the blanket, the globes of the bedposts, the cloying warmth of the pillow.

At the foot of the bed, she finds a pile of coarse wool. Her cloak?

She runs a finger over the hem, following it up over lines of hooks and buttons. Yes, she remembers. She had been at the inn before she had been attacked. Had been speaking with Bessie in the room full of flowers. She had left her cloak draped over a chair.

She digs a hand into the pocket. The letter Asher Hales had given her is there. The letter that had told her Jacob Bailey had abandoned his family. She does not take it out. Best that cursed thing stays hidden.

She tosses the cloak back over the foot of the bed. She cannot just lie here and hope. Cannot just pray for the light, or for the safe return of her brother's children. She had been the last one to see them. Had held them in her arms while their mother lay unconscious at her feet.

She tries to think. Tries to remember.

Air moving against her cheek. She had been struck from behind. Had had no chance to see who was in the cave with them. But there must be something in her memories; some sound, some smell, some hint at who had been there.

Think. Remember.

But there is nothing. Nothing to remember beyond the white hot pain that had taken her sight away.

The dark shifts and sways around her. Where is Flora? Scarlett needs to not be alone.

The rooms around her are quiet. She hears a table groan as it is pushed along the floor in the tavern below.

She climbs out of bed. Runs a hand along the wall until she

reaches the doorway. She knows the inn well. This is the first guestroom. That way is the parlour. And here; the top of the stairs. She feels the floor fall away beneath the tips of her toes.

"Scarlett—" Flora's voice is sharp. "Stay there."

No. She feels the stair rail beneath her hand, worn smooth, just as she remembers. There is something faintly comforting about it. The world she knows is still here. Slowly, carefully, she steps down into the bar. The familiar scent of beeswax polish rises to meet her. Her hand slides off the end of the bannister.

"You ought to be resting," says Flora. She pushes aside Scarlett's hair to inspect the gash on the back of her head.

No, she ought to be out there helping Isaac and Caroline find their children. Ought to be out there punishing whoever had attacked her.

The pale sun on her cheek tells her it is morning. A full day since she had arrived from Portreath and walked down the hill into Talland.

She ought to be in Polperro, saying goodbye to the man who had brought her home.

Jamie will know nothing, of course, of all that has happened. He will know nothing of the attack in the cave or the missing children or the eternal darkness that has fallen over her. He will just see that she has not come to say goodbye. He will think his role in the revenue service has been enough to turn her away.

Her throat tightens.

"At least sit down," says Flora, leading her to a chair.

Scarlett sits. A shawl is tossed around her shoulders. Never in her life has she felt so useless.

This cannot be forever.

"You can help me, can't you, Flora? You know how to fix

this, ayes? You know what to do."

Flora doesn't answer at once. Her silence makes Scarlett's stomach roll.

"Answer me," she says, sharper than she had intended. "You can help me, can't you."

And Flora says: "Of course."

Of course, she'd said. *Of course I can help.*

When Scarlett goes back to bed to rest, Flora finds herself pacing the room that had once been Jack's. Leaves are strung up across the mantle to dry, filling the place with the scent of the moors. She runs a finger along them, feeling their damp, velvety softness.

Of course I can help.

What else was there to say? How could she have admitted she has no idea where to begin?

Her head is full of tonics and incantations. Cures for coughs and colds, snake-bites and scurvy. Charms for luck and to keep the devil at bay.

But a cure for lost sight? Flora is not even sure such a thing is possible.

Her mother would have believed it was. Her mother had believed everything could be cured with concoctions and prayer and whispered incantations. But for all the steps Flora has taken to immerse herself in the world of the craft, her faith is precarious at best.

She empties the contents of her mother's chest onto the floor. There are pouches of angelica and mallow and lengths of hangman's rope. The black mirror, wrapped in a cloth so it might hide its secrets. There is little that will be of any help to Scarlett.

Had her mother felt this same uselessness, Flora wonders? Had she held herself responsible each time her incantations had failed to save a life?

Her mother had not been a good healer. All the faith in the world had not stopped men dying with her charms in their hands. Flora had grown more critical of the craft each time another body was lowered into their churchyard.

But there is no time now for criticism or doubt.

She tries to think. Tries to sift through her memories for any charm that might be of use.

Crowfoot, the kenning herb, for ulcers of the eyes.

It won't work. She feels it inside her.

But she has trained herself to offer cures with conviction. And she knows Scarlett is a believer. She will trust the crowfoot can bring back the light. And that, Flora is sure, has to be worth something.

She puts everything back into the chest and goes out to the hallway. She will try with the crowfoot when Scarlett has had a little more rest.

Two of the old guestrooms opened. Flora has sifted through the belongings of her mother, her husband. Only one more room to open. She can't remember the last time she had seen its door unlocked.

Her father had been a merchant sailor who had spent months on end at sea. In his long absences, she and her mother had lost themselves in a world of fragrant, bubbling teas and mirrors.

His death had been a sudden thing, a week after Flora's ninth birthday. Her most vivid memories of the man are of him lying dead on the floor in that locked-up room. One moment he had been replacing a loose floorboard, the next, lying on his back, staring at the rugged beams of the roof. Flora remembers crouching beside his body, eyes fixed on the pale threads of hair beneath the open laces of his shirt. She had tried to imagine the still heart that lay beneath.

It had been after her father's burial, she supposes, that her mother had locked the door. Had she hidden his things away in there to try and stem her grief?

After her father's death, Flora's life had gone on much the way it had when he'd been alive. There will be little sentimentality when she opens that door. None of the gentle grief she had felt when she had sifted through her mother and husband's things. Just a vague sense of pity for a man she had barely known.

But there is a reluctance in her, nonetheless.

She is opening these rooms so she can put guests inside them. This has been her plan from the very beginning. But the closer she gets to such a thing, the more uncomfortable it makes her.

She will open the tavern to the people of Talland, yes. But the top floors of the inn have always been her home. She had been born in these rooms. Had stitched her wedding dress, become a mother. It feels wrong to let strangers traipse their way through such precious memories.

But she has little choice. Because now, with the shelves bare of liquor and the excisemen's eyes on her, the Mariner's Arms is nothing but a languishing alehouse. Soon, the men who have bought her lambswool in an act of charity will have a thirst for rum and brandy she'll not be able to satisfy. Her only hope of survival is to fill the place with overnight guests. Have strangers' footsteps echoing down her halls.

Sighing to herself, she pulls the ring of keys from the

drawer in the parlour. She carries it back to the locked room.

Which key?

Each jams in the lock and refuses to turn. Flora tries once more, then makes her way back to the parlour and tosses the keys into the drawer.

She tried, she tells herself. What more is there to do?

RUINS

She is not coming.

Jamie has waited throughout the morning. He has done so many circuits of Polperro he'll be seeing these whitewashed cottages in his dreams. It is well past noon. His horse is growing restless at being saddled and unridden.

Winter is close and dusk will come early. He needs to leave now if he is to make it to Truro before dark.

He has been here far longer than he intended. Had promised Scarlett he would return to Portreath the moment he knew she had made it home safely. Promised her he would turn his back. Not peek beneath the surface into her life of smuggling.

Resting the horse, he had told her, as an explanation for his staying. Resting the horse and himself. There had been an element of truth to it. He and Scarlett had ridden across the county in less than two days. They had spent a night in a Truro inn, Jamie kept awake by the snoring of eight other men in the dormitory around him. By the time they had reached Talland, he had been craving sleep. But there had also been a reluctance in him to leave her.

He'd spent the night at the Three Pilchards, close to Polperro harbour. Had stared at the ceiling until dawn, listening to ratlines clatter in the dark. He can count on one hand the hours of sleep he's had since Scarlett Bailey had barrelled into his life.

He'd lay there with his thoughts full of her. He knew well how foolish this was. He was an officer of the revenue service. She, the woman he had caught with her hands in a chest of smuggled tobacco. He ought never have ridden to Talland with her. Ought to have given her money for a coach ride home and wished her the best of luck. A far more sensible course of action. But sense, Jamie is coming to realise, is something he seems to have in short supply of late.

And so, today, she has not come. Today, she has been wiser than him. She has seen it is best to end this now, before he becomes anything more than the man who had seen her home.

There is a dull ache in his chest as he swings himself onto his horse. For the best.

He tells himself again. *For the best.*

He begins to ride. Suddenly he wants nothing more than to be gone from this place. He wants to be back in Portreath, patrolling the cliffs on horseback while the sea curls beneath him. He wants windblown hair and rain-soaked clothes, wants the thunder of hooves rattling his body. He wants to hide in watch houses to catch smugglers in the act, wants to comb the cliffs to find the men hiding beneath.

And this is what she is, he reminds himself, as Polperro slips into the valley. Scarlett Bailey is the woman willing to run smuggled tobacco to the men on the hills. She is midnight landings and silent deliveries and the secret language of the signalling lanterns. Reminding himself makes this easier. She is all the things he has committed himself to eradicating.

The last patches of blue disappear from the sky as he follows the road into rusty moorland. A cold wind swirls, catching hold of the ends of his scarf.

He will head west, make for the river. Follow it north until he finds the road to Truro. He will retrace the journey he and Scarlett had made from Portreath; a windswept trek past tors and barrows and ice-flecked streams.

She'd spent most of the ride talking. Her reluctance to have him accompany her home was gone before Portreath had vanished behind the hills.

"What's your horse's name?" she'd asked.

He said: "Scarlett."

She laughed. "You're making that up." She looked over her shoulder at him. "Are you making that up?"

Yes, he said, he was making it up. He told her of how he'd purchased the horse from a Portreath farmer and had named her Arrow, for the markings on her flank. He told her of teaching himself to ride on his grandfather's farm, of the enormous black horse in his *sira-wynn*'s stables that had terrified him when he was a boy.

She had chattered about her years in the children's home, and the excitement she had felt when her brother had appeared to take her back to Talland. She told him of her niece and nephew and her cottage on the hill. Days pressing and salting at the pilchard palace, nights serving ale at the village tavern.

She leant back against his chest and Jamie felt his heart quicken.

Later, she told him of the letter she had been given, claiming her father had been hiding in Portreath.

He knew of her father, of course, the bastard who'd been up to his eyes in illegal impressment. When she'd begun to speak of him, Jamie had found himself changing the subject.

They had talked for two days without drawing breath, yet had managed to dance around enormous chunks of their lives. He knew nothing of how deep she and her family was in the world of smuggling. And he'd told her no details of his appointment to the revenue service two years earlier. Told her nothing of the patrols, the watches, the trials he had been involved in to see smuggling syndicates unravelled and free traders carted off in chains.

There'd been an unspoken understanding between them. Topics too difficult to raise. A bridge too fragile to cross.

The roads are empty and thick with mud. The river slices the earth, silver and sighing.

Jamie crosses the bridge. Sees the skeleton of a castle blotting the sky. The ruins are otherworldly in the half light. He turns up the collar of his coat, shivering as he rides past.

He and his brother had been raised by their grandmother, a woman with an endless supply of ghostly tales and legends. She had believed the stories unquestionably, had told them in whispers while the fire hissed and rain pattered against the glass. His earliest memories are of curling up beneath the bedclothes listening to tales of haunted ruins. Relics populated by grey ladies and silent, vanishing monks.

Jamie looks up at the castle shell. It is round and low, built on a faint rise of the earth. One side of the grey stone wall is little more than rubble. There is a prickly energy to the place, as though fragments of the past still linger.

He continues riding. Such places have always unnerved him.

At the edge of his vision, he sees something move in the ruins. He stops the horse. Looks again at the castle. Such places have always unnerved him, but they also hold his curiosity.

He waits. Hears the wings of a gull beat above his head. And there it is again, clearer this time. A flash of movement within the keep. He sees a man with dark hair tangled around his shoulders. Jamie sees only the back of his head as he darts through the shadows. The figure is gone so quickly he is unsure whether he had seen anything at all.

He takes the horse closer. Watches the animal for any reaction, any sense of the otherworldly. The horse turns up its ears. And a sound comes on the wind. The cry of a baby.

Jamie almost laughs. In the ghost stories his grandmother had told, there was always the cry of a baby.

He waits. There is no more crying. There is no sound at all, but the distant burble of the river. It had been nothing but his imagination, surely.

He ought to ride away. The place makes the hair on the back of his neck stand on end.

But as he turns to leave, he hears murmuring. Men's voices.

Jamie hesitates. He has hunted down free traders in graveyards, found ankers stored in coffins, hauled contraband out of empty wells.

He knows an abandoned castle is a fine place for smugglers to hide their goods.

The thing about this life, Jamie had come to realise when he'd first begun to patrol the coast, was that it was impossible to stop looking. Stop suspecting, stop doubting, stop guessing. This journey was supposed to be about nothing more than seeing Scarlett home safely. And yet he has his uniform and journal in his saddle bag, his pistol in his pocket. How can he stop looking in a place where smuggling is as natural as breathing?

He glances again at the castle.

He had promised Scarlett he would ride away and not ask questions. Had not imagined keeping his word would be so difficult.

So here are his choices: approach the castle and uncover a potential smugglers' haul. Or ride away, keeping his promise to a woman who had not seen fit to say goodbye.

Ride away. A promise is a promise.

If there are smugglers in the castle they may well be a part of the Baileys' syndicate.

The shot comes before he has a chance to move. It flies over his shoulder and sends his horse bolting across the moor. He grapples with the reins to avoid being thrown. When the horse begins to calm, he gently slows her, fumbling in his pocket for the pistol. Riding away from murmuring men is one thing, but to hell if he'll turn his back when there are shots flying over his shoulder.

He climbs from the saddle, lowering himself slowly to the ground to avoid making a sound. He glances around him. There is nowhere to tether the horse, but the bent skeleton of a tree. He loops the reins around a gnarled grey branch, hoping it will hold.

He draws in his breath, pushing his dark hair out of his eyes. The castle rises ahead of him. To his left, the gate that had once held the drawbridge gapes.

He cannot enter this way. The shooter will be expecting it.

He follows the wall until he finds a place dilapidated enough for him to climb through.

Inside is silent. The castle roof is long-vanished and clouds hang low over the crumbling ruins. Jamie's breath makes a cloud in front of him.

He grips his gun. His heart is thudding. The footsteps, the fleeting image of the man, the crying child, they had felt otherworldly. But the gunshot— that had been real.

He walks carefully, silently, keeping to the patches of grass that poke between the stone.

He can smell horses. Where are they hidden? There are plenty of rooms still intact enough for a man to hide his animal.

He finds them in the shell of the great hall. Two dark grey horses, shifting restlessly in the shadows. They are saddled, their reins looped to an outward-jutting piece of stone. There is no sign of any contraband.

Jamie continues along the edge of the courtyard until he is back at the hole through which he had entered.

There is nothing. Not a sound from this world, or another. No sign of men, or smuggled goods. Whoever had been here has left.

He makes his way out of the hole in the castle wall and across the indent left by the long-empty moat. The men have not taken their horses. They cannot be far. But the light is beginning to drain and shadows lie thick over the moor. He sees no sign of movement, beyond his horse silhouetted in the distance. The tree branch to which he had tied her lies broken on the ground.

He walks slowly towards the horse, crooning and murmuring to keep her from bolting. He lurches for the reins and runs a hand down the velvety plane of her nose.

Then he goes back to the castle. Waits for the men to return for their horses.

He sits in the saddle for two hours or more. There is no

one.

He shivers. He is exhausted and shaken. Will not make it to Truro by dark. It would be foolish, he knows, to ride any further north tonight. Best he return to Polperro.

He hesitates. He had promised Scarlett he would not stay.

But whatever had been between them is over and done. Surely she cannot begrudge him a safe night's sleep.

He tugs on the reins and heads back towards the village.

THE DOMAIN OF DESPERATE MEN

"I heard about the children," Martha Francis says, appearing at the cottage door with an elaborately wrapped saffron cake. "I'm so dreadfully sorry."

Caroline doesn't look up from the carrots she is slicing. Eating is the last thing she feels like doing, but she and Isaac have agreed to force down a little supper. She knows they will need to keep up their strength if they are to continue searching at the rate they have been. She has spent the day questioning villagers in Killigarth and her eyes are heavy with exhaustion.

Isaac gives Martha a nod of thanks, gesturing for her to enter.

Caroline grits her teeth. Eating is the last thing she feels like doing, closely followed by indulging Martha Francis. Her knife slams rhythmically into the chopping board. A slice of carrot flies across the kitchen.

Martha sets the cake on the table. "You need to go to the forest," she says fervently. "You need to go after them."

Caroline looks up. "What? Go after who?"

"The piskeys, of course. The fairies." Martha turns to Isaac. "You know this was their doing, don't you?"

Caroline feels something sink inside her. The brief moment of hope gives way to anger. She puts down the knife and closes her eyes.

Isaac ushers the old woman back towards the door. "Martha, please. It's not a good time."

"You know I'm right, Isaac," she says, winding her apron around a gnarled finger. "I know you've not forgotten everything your mother taught you. You know there are spirits out there we ought to be afraid of. Spirits that are more than capable of taking your children."

"I've not forgotten," Isaac says, impatience on the edge of his voice. "I just think our time could be better spent looking elsewhere."

Martha sighs, shaking her head in frustration. She looks over Isaac's shoulder at Caroline. "You ought to have pinned her to the crib."

Caroline's eyes flash. "What?"

"Young Mary. You ought to have pinned her nightgown to the crib. It's what I used to do with my Will. Only way to stop the fairy folk from taking them."

Caroline charges out from behind the table. "Get out!" she cries. "Get out of my house with these ridiculous stories!" She slams the door as Martha bustles over the doorstep. The thud of it rattles her insides. She chews her thumbnail. "She's blaming me," she says, beginning to pace in front of the hearth. "She thinks me a bad mother."

Isaac takes her shoulders and holds her against him. "No one is blaming you."

"Did you not hear her? I ought to have pinned Mary's

47

nightgown…"

"Ignore her. She obviously doesn't know the full story."

Caroline shrugs out of his grip. "I'm done with this place," she says bitterly. "I'm done living among people who cannot see sense." Once, she had welcomed these tales. They had brought a flicker of magic to a life that had been devoid of anything close. What harm would it do, she had thought, to imagine for a moment that piskeys danced on rooftops and giants walked the earth. But the allure of myths and fairy tales had worn thin many years ago.

Isaac plays with the lacy edge of the cloth wrapped around the saffron cake. "It's just how these people are," he says gently. "These stories are how they cope. How they make sense of the world."

Caroline throws the carrots into the pot and hangs it over the stove. "These stories are not going to help us find our children."

With supper forced down, Isaac goes back out to search. Caroline stands in the doorway and watches him leave. Wind stings her cheeks and thrashes her skirts around her legs. Bends the trees towards the sea.

She stays motionless for a long time. She cannot go back inside. The emptiness of the place is stifling. Go inside and she will find herself staring at the door of the nursery, thinking of the disused bed, the rumpled blankets, the empty cradle swaying in the draught.

Go inside and she will find herself staring into the room she shares with her husband. She will wonder how many nights he has lain beside her, wishing he were somewhere else.

She had had her suspicions, of course. Had told herself

they would amount to nothing. She had not wanted to believe her husband capable of such things.

But how can she be angry when her betrayal is so much worse? How many nights does she have left to lie beside him before her secrets unravel completely?

The pain, the anger, the fear of it is too much.

A figure moves through the darkness.

Jacob Bailey is striding down the hill towards the cottage. Caroline races towards him. There is a tirade on her lips, but Jacob speaks first.

"Why are you still here?"

"Do you honestly think this is the way to get me to leave?" she cries. "Do you expect me to disappear from this place without knowing my children are safe?" She hurries inside, away from the prying eyes of the village. Slams the door behind Jacob.

His eyes dart around the cottage, taking it in. This had been his home too, Caroline remembers. He had sat at her table, made fires in her hearth, slept in her bed.

She sinks into a chair and rubs her eyes in resigned exhaustion. "Tell him," she coughs. "Tell Isaac everything. I just want my children back. They can't suffer for my mistakes." She hears the waver in her voice. She doesn't care. Let Jacob win.

He hovers over her, a frown deepening the creases in his leathery brow. "Something has happened to your children?"

Surprise in his voice?

No, he is playing with her. He is the one who has done this, Caroline is sure. He has done it to punish her, to force her to leave. To put her through the same pain she had inflicted on him.

"Just tell me where they are," she says. "Please."

But something has softened in Jacob's face. His lips are pursed beneath the grey mess of his beard. "What happened?" he asks.

Caroline sees something in his eyes. Something she has seen in her husband's eyes. That desperation to protect his family. This, she remembers, is the man who had exiled himself to save his wife and daughter's lives.

The realisation swings at her suddenly. Whoever had taken the children had attacked Scarlett to do it. Jacob Bailey would kill a man in cold blood and set up another to take the blame. He would steal, he would lie, and he would risk his crewmates' lives for his own gain.

But he would not harm the daughter he had done everything to protect.

"It wasn't you," she says.

"Of course not."

Caroline begins to gnaw on her thumbnail. "I believed you," she says. "On the beach. I believed you when you said you'd hurt Mary."

Jacob turns away. "She's Isaac's child. I'd never lay a finger on her."

Caroline's thoughts race. She had been sure Jacob was responsible. She had watched Isaac charge up Reuben's front path and been certain he would find nothing. She is not sure whether this revelation makes her terrified or relieved. But Jacob Bailey is not the only one seeking to bring her down. He is not the only man she wishes she had never met. How much can she continue to hide when her children's lives are in danger?

She pins Jacob with cold eyes. "Where is Asher Hales?"

This feels like the greatest of mistakes. The domain of desperate men.

Asher crouches at the edge of the river and scoops a handful of murky water into his mouth. He winces, tasting mud. The light has faded and the trees around him are thick silhouettes. He has planted a lamp in the muck of the riverbank, and the water ripples orange in the glow of the flame.

He looks up at the sound of approaching hooves. Tom Leach is in the saddle, leading a second horse by the reins. They are fine grey mares, stolen from a farm on the outskirts of Polperro.

They were to hide, Leach had said, in the ruins of Restormel Castle. He had been sheltering there alone since he had run from Polruan and the authorities almost a week earlier.

The castle had been a good place to shelter. Silent and ghostly, surrounded by nothing but empty moorland. Cover from the wind and river water to drink.

But this afternoon Leach had seen a man approaching. Shots had been fired. The silence and safety of the castle broken.

Involving himself with this reckless man, Asher sees now, had been the greatest of mistakes.

But two nights ago he had sat at the edge of Polperro harbour and watched Caroline walk back over the hill to Isaac. The woman he loved was to leave this place with her husband, taking with her the knowledge of how to find Henry Avery's haul. Money Asher had spent half his life searching for.

He had been on the verge of giving up. His dreams of becoming a wealthy, educated surgeon felt unreachable. Caroline was right. He'd never be anything more than a desperate fool.

And then there was Tom Leach, standing over him at the edge of the harbour. Asher had seen something of a kindred spirit. Lost men. Shunned and scorned.

Leach had asked questions and Asher had found himself answering. Had spilled all he knew about Caroline's desire to leave Talland.

Leach paced. "When?" he asked. And: "How do they mean to get past Reuben?"

To each; *I don't know.*

Asher knew he had nothing. No reliable information. No way to stop Caroline from disappearing. No way to resurrect his glittering future, his longed-for dreams.

"They can't leave," Leach said, staring across the anchorage to the dark shape of Isaac's lugger. "I'll not let it happen." He kept staring. He was making plans, Asher could tell.

"You're a wanted man," he told Leach finally, more to fill the silence than anything else. "Why are you here?" But as he spoke, he began to see.

Two riding officers had been killed in Lansallos. Tom Leach the prime suspect. He had returned to this place to punish Isaac for turning him over to the authorities. He was making plans to stop the Baileys from escaping. And Asher Hales needed to be a part of them.

"Tell me what you're planning," he said. "I can help you." He pressed his shoulders back, lifted his chin. He knew he looked a sorry creature; his face bruised and swollen, his clothes grimy and splattered with old blood. But he wanted

Leach to see the man he was beneath. Wanted him to see that Asher Hales was a fine person with whom to share a secret.

"Their children," Leach said finally. "We'll take them."

Asher swallowed. He didn't know he had been expecting, but it wasn't this.

Take Caroline's children? Did he have it in him to deliver such brutality? A big part of him doubted it. But he saw the brilliance of the plan. With Caroline's children beneath his arms, he would have power. He would speak and she would listen. Be swayed. Manipulated.

She would tell him where Henry Avery's money was hidden. And she would leave this place on his arm, to build the life they had planned. She would have no choice. No leverage. Her children for her secrets.

Asher managed a small nod.

Leach raked long fingers through his beard. "In the morning," he said, "when Isaac has gone to sea, you'll go to the cottage and take the children from their mother. Bring them here. I'll have a boat waiting."

Me? Asher thought to say. *No. I couldn't...* He wanted to be involved, yes. But he didn't want to be the one with blood on his hands.

But he saw the pistol tucked in Leach's pocket. Saw the wildness in his eyes. This man was a killer. If the tales were to be believed, he had murdered two revenue officers at close range. He could not let this man anywhere near Caroline.

And so over the cliff path to Talland Asher walked, a man following orders. He hated the way such a thing felt. And yet he was so drained and weary, that acting on his own accord had begun to feel like an impossibility. He had been making plans for more than half his life. Had never seen any of them become reality. Why not let someone else carry the burden for once?

When he reached Talland, the village was still blanketed in darkness. He sat on the edge of the road, staring up at the Baileys' lightless cottage.

He ought to act now. Force open the window and take the children from their beds. What was the alternative? Take them in broad daylight from beneath Caroline's nose? Such a thing would require force, violence.

He couldn't. What kind of man would raise a hand to the woman he loved?

Act now.

His legs were heavy with reluctance, his thoughts sluggish and dull.

He sat staring at the cottage until dawn. He watched Isaac leave for the fishing port, watched farmers wheel carts of vegetables over the hill towards the market.

Watched Scarlett appear from the top of the hill.

Asher scrambled from the road and hid himself in the copse of trees opposite the cottage.

She stopped outside the front door, knotting her fingers together. Then she walked back down the road towards the church.

Enough hesitating. It had to be now.

Asher stepped out from his hiding place and crept closer to the cottage. Through the window, he could see Caroline racing across the house, shoving clothes into a trunk that sat in the middle of the kitchen.

How was he to go about this? He had no weapon with which to threaten her. Even if he had, she knew him well enough to know he would never have the courage to use it.

And here came men striding up the hill from the direction of the Mariner's Arms. Men Asher had seen before. Men working for Charles Reuben.

He watched as they forced their way into the cottage.

Muffled shouts. Crashes and thuds. And as quickly as they had arrived, the men were gone.

Out they came from the house; Caroline and the children. They were dressed for travel, a chaos of cloaks and scarves and hats. Had disappeared over the cliff path before Asher could make sense of it.

He followed.

At the top of the hill he stopped and looked down into the village. There was Caroline, hurrying towards the cliff-rimmed harbour. Behind the jagged wall of rock, Asher knew Tom Leach was waiting with his stolen dory.

It had been more than an hour since Isaac had left for the fishing port. How long would it be before Leach declared Asher a failure and went after the children himself?

Caroline waded through the shallow water on the edge of the beach, a hand around her son's wrist, the baby pinned against her hip. She ushered the boy into the cave. What was she doing? Seeking shelter from Reuben and his men? This, Asher felt certain, was not the secret, underhand escape Isaac and Caroline had planned.

He ought to go to her, he thought distantly. Ought to tell her that Leach was waiting on the sea. Ought to tell her the cave she was sheltering in was not by safe water.

But go to Caroline and he would open himself up to Leach's wrath. The thought of being on the wrong side of that animal was terrifying.

He sat on the edge of the cliff and watched the dizzying roll of the sea. Let Isaac fight Tom Leach. No doubt they had been working towards it for years.

He let his eyes grow glassy. Let the sea blur. Was this guilt he was feeling? Self-loathing? His thoughts were tangled.

Once his mind had been so sharp. He'd questioned and analysed and worked tirelessly to unravel the riddles of the world around him. He'd studied every inch of the human body, inside and out, had hypothesised on the intangible magic of the soul. Asher Hales had been a man destined to make his imprint on the world.

He laughed aloud. That man had been beaten out of existence.

Here was Scarlett again, charging towards him, yanking him out of his stupor.

"Was this your doing?" she cried. "Did you go to the revenue men? Is that why my family has left?"

She was a mess; her clothes dripping with seawater, skirts tangled around her legs. Dark threads of hair clung to her flushed cheeks.

"What are you talking about, Scarlett?"

"Did you see my brother's ship leave?" she asked, her voice strained and desperate.

"He left, yes. With the fishing fleet. This morning."

"With the fishing fleet? Did it seem as though he were coming back?"

Asher laughed humourlessly. "Here you are wanting my help again." To hell with her. He would not let himself be threatened by Scarlett Bailey any longer.

"Tell me what you saw, Asher! I need to know if my family has left!"

How like her father she was, with her flashing eyes and violent temper. Could she see the resemblance?

He let out an enormous sigh and looked back out across the sea. "She is leaving, yes. And taking with her all she knows."

"What?" Scarlett demanded. "Who are you talking about? Caroline?"

"She knows," he said distantly. "She knows how to find the money."

"What are you talking about? What money? Avery's money?"

Asher nodded faintly. He was dimly aware that this secret was not his to reveal. Dimly aware of how much Caroline's life would unravel if he kept speaking. But if her life were to unravel, she would have nowhere to turn but to him.

Scarlett, in her frantic state was unable to catch hold of the threads he was dangling. "You're making no sense, Asher," she snapped, looking at him as though he were a madman.

Little Scarlett Bailey with a knife at her knee. Let her go to Leach. Let her try and stop him. It would be a fine thing to see.

"They're in the cave," he told her. "Your family. I saw them."

Asher feels himself tense as Leach slides from the horse. It had been a welcome respite to have him return to the castle for the animals. It is a difficult thing to relax, Asher is coming to realise, when in the company of Tom Leach.

He glances over his shoulder at the children. They are asleep on the ratty saddle blanket he had tossed on the ground, the boy on his side, the baby curled up against his stomach. They are a mess of grimy clothes and tangled hair, suffused with the stench of river muck and shit.

Leach lashes the horses to a tree. He glances at the children, then at Asher. "Kill them."

Asher looks down. The easiest option, perhaps. And, he sees now, it was what Leach had intended to do from the

57

beginning. What better punishment for Isaac Bailey?

In the end, Asher had followed Scarlett down to the cave. At the end of all this, there would be Caroline, and there would be money. Go through with this brutal plan and it would lead him to the life he had always wanted.

He stood at the mouth of the cave and held his breath. Caroline lay on the sand with a line of blood running from the side of her head. Sickness rose in Asher's throat. He wanted to kneel at her side, help her awaken and promise her everything would be all right. But Leach stood less than a foot away, a long metal creeping pole in his hand.

Scarlett was crouching at the back of the cave, speaking under her breath to the children. Asher watched as Leach raised the pole and swung; a fierce blow to the back of Scarlett's head. The crack filled the cave and brought a sound from Asher's throat.

Scarlett fell close to his feet. Leach yanked the children out from the gap in the rock, a hand over the boy's mouth to muffle his screams. He shoved them at Asher. At the kicking, shrieking weight of them in his arms, the reality of what they were doing swung at him. But it was too late to turn back. The thing was done.

He clamped a hand over the boy's mouth, unsure what else to do.

Leach marched from the cave without looking back. "The boat is waiting around the point."

"Kill them," Leach says again. He tosses Asher the pistol. It feels heavy in his hands.

Asher looks down at the gun. He has no food for them. No shelter now their hideout at the castle has been discovered. The brandy bottle he has been using to drug them both into a stupor is dangerously close to empty.

"They're precious leverage," he tells Leach. "Without them, we have nothing."

The baby sighs and murmurs in her sleep. Asher feels a tug of regret. The mewling of Caroline's daughter was supposed to come from the nursery in their grand Belgravia townhouse, not some filthy saddle blanket here at the end of the earth.

He needs to get to her. Tell her the children are safe and will be back in her arms the moment she agrees to his wishes.

But just how safe are they? Leach's pistol is loaded. The situation, Asher is beginning to realise, is slipping from his control. Perhaps it had never been in his control.

He flings the gun back towards Leach. It thuds heavily on the earth.

"Take them then," Leach says dismissively. "You want to keep them alive, you do it somewhere else."

Asher glances at the children. They cannot spend another night out in the cold. They might never wake from their sleep.

But where is he to go? He has no money, no food, no clean clothes. He is as much of an outcast as Leach.

"Your house in Polruan," he says suddenly. "Let me use it."

Leach snorts. "You're not using my house."

"Why not?"

"Because my wife is in it. And I don't want her dealing with the likes of you."

Asher snorts. If Leach's wife has any wit to her she will have run the moment her husband had disappeared. Gone some place he could never find her.

But he says nothing. Because when Leach speaks of his wife there is a look in his eyes Asher has not seen before. A look that is almost concern, almost affection.

Asher climbs to his feet. His boots sink into the mud on the edge of the river. "Let me take the children there, just for the night. I can tell her you're safe. Alive." Would the woman care, he wonders? But he says: "She's worried for you, I'm sure."

Leach looks at him without speaking. Finally, he gives a short nod. He picks up his pistol and tucks it back in his pocket.

Asher hunches over the boy and shakes his shoulder. He blinks, then his dark eyes widen, as though remembering where he is.

"Get up," says Asher. "We're leaving."

The boy scrambles to his feet. Stumbles. There is still brandy in his blood. "Where are we going?"

"Somewhere you'll be warm."

Asher looks down at the baby, unsure quite what to do with her. The boy plucks her from the ground and holds her tight against his chest. She gives Asher a slow, brown-eyed blink, then stuffs her mouth full of her brother's hair.

Asher swallows heavily and gestures towards the horse.

Leach pulls the remains of the brandy from the pack. "Go to Caroline Bailey and I'll kill you." He tilts the bottle, watching its contents run up the side of the glass. "She and her husband can't know their children are alive. Let them suffer."

Asher says nothing. He hauls the boy onto the horse, then climbs into the saddle behind him. Gabriel grips the pommel with one hand, his other arm wrapped around his squalling sister.

Asher rides by moonlight, out of the thick forest and onto the muddy road that will take them to the coast. The boy's head turns from side to side as they walk. He is sharp-eyed, quick. Asher is not surprised by it. He is half Caroline.

He goads the horse into a canter, to quell any thoughts of escape.

Gabriel looks over his shoulder at Asher. The boy recognises him from the days he had spent at their cottage, he can tell.

"Aunt Scarlett says you almost drowned."

The mention of Scarlett brings a faint tug to Asher's chest. She had saved his life. And in return, he had led her into the cave where Leach and his creeping pole had been waiting.

"What is it like?" asks Gabriel, looking out over the dark plain of the sea. "Being shipwrecked? Did you hear the voices in the wind? Did they call your name? Did you think you were going to die?"

The night is thick by the time they reach Polruan, sparse stars speckling the cloud bank. Asher leads the horse through the winding streets, following the directions Leach had given.

The baby has begun to cry again, fraying Asher's nerves. He hauls the children from the horse and knocks on the door of Leach's cottage. It is answered by a young woman in a patched grey dress and apron. Strands of orange hair peek out from beneath her cap, grazing a soft, freckled face. Her blue eyes are enormous.

"You're Tom Leach's wife?" Asher asks in surprise. "Jane?" He had been expecting someone older, someone harsher, someone with the same ferocity in her eyes as her husband.

She eyes him warily, then looks at the children. The boy is staring up at her, the baby a grizzling, kicking mess.

"Who are you?" Jane asks Asher.

"Your husband sent me."

"You've seen Tom? Is he safe? Where is he?"

Truly? Such concern for the man? Such innocent, wide-eyed worry? What has Tom Leach ever done to deserve such things?

"He's safe," Asher tells the woman. "For now."

"Where is he?" she presses. When Asher doesn't answer, she twists a finger around the edge of her apron. "Are these your children?"

Doesn't she know better than to ask questions? Doesn't she know who her husband is?

Asher nudges Gabriel into the house. "Tom wants you to take care of them," he lies.

She nods stiffly, then kneels so she is eye level with the boy. He looks at her distrustfully, his arms tightening around the baby.

"Is this your sister?" Jane asks gently.

He nods.

"May I take her?"

He hesitates. "She's scared."

"I know." Jane's voice is soft, despite Mary's wailing. "Let me help."

Finally, Gabriel loosens his grip and lets Jane lift the baby into her arms. She rubs Mary's back and speaks to Gabriel in words Asher can't hear. Then she ushers him into another room.

Asher hovers in the doorway, feeling an intruder. Not knowing what else to do, he steps inside. A fire is crackling in the hearth, underskirts hanging over the guard to dry. A single plate sits in the middle of the table, scattered with breadcrumbs.

Asher goes to the fire. He reaches over the guard and holds his hands close to the flames. He feels chilled to the core.

When the children return, their faces have been wiped

clean, the twigs and grass combed from their dark hair. The baby smells far less eye-wateringly foul.

Jane bustles around the kitchen with Mary on her hip, pulling bread from the shelf and filling a saucepan with milk. She hangs the pot over the fire and places a plate of bread and cheese in front of Gabriel. She smooths his hair. Murmurs more unintelligible words.

Finally, she looks back at Asher. "And who exactly are you?" she asks.

He says: "Matthew Fielding." It feels fitting to give his old, tarnished name. Asher Hales was supposed to be a new name for a new man. And he has never felt further from that man.

Jane watches Gabriel stuff the cheese into his mouth. He's had nothing but a few scraps of stale bread in days, Asher realises, feeling a faint stab of guilt.

"Tom took these children?" Jane asks under her breath. "Why?"

Asher finds himself tugging at the laces of his shirt. A nervous habit that had developed around the time he had begun to involve himself with Tom Leach. He forces his hands into his lap. "He wants revenge against the man he believes turned him in for murder."

Jane's jaw tightens. Her eyes move over him, scrutinising. Then, as though she has decided he is not worth the attention, she goes to the hearth and pours the milk into two tin cups. She passes one to Gabriel. Sits the baby on her lap and drizzles the warm liquid into her mouth.

Asher glances about him for any evidence of other children. He sees nothing.

He eyes the plate of bread and cheese. He is hungry too. But asking to be fed feels like a step too far.

Tomorrow he will go to Caroline. Put an end to this. To

hell with what Tom Leach wants. He has followed the man's orders too long already.

The thought of going against Leach's wishes makes Asher edgy. Nervous. But Tom Leach is a wanted man. He has no leverage. He has nothing. Asher will get what he wants from this whole sorry exercise. Somehow, he will wrangle his life back onto the course it ought to have taken.

The chair squeaks noisily as he takes a seat at the table. Gabriel shoots him a distrusting look, then turns back to his food.

"Tomorrow," Asher tells him, his voice coming out softer than he had intended. "Tomorrow you'll see your mother."

THE GIRL WITH LIGHT FINGERS

Jamie comes downstairs from his room at the Three Pilchards. His legs are weighted and his eyes heavy. He holds up a hand to shield his eyes from a violent spear of morning light. He orders strong coffee and sits at the bar with his hands wrapped around the mug.

At the other end of the counter, sits a man he recognises. Jamie had sent him away from the press gang's cart shed before the riding officers had made their arrests. Scarlett's father is staring out the window, sipping from a shallow tin cup.

Why is he here? Has he come after his daughter?

Jamie knows he ought to walk away. Scarlett has made it clear there is to be nothing more between them. What good will it do to approach her criminal of a father? But he has been kept awake by thoughts of Scarlett Bailey for too many nights now for him to walk away. He tosses back the last of his coffee and approaches the man.

He eyes Jamie warily. "You. What are you doing in this

place?"

So the man remembers him. Remembers the way he had sent his fellow riding officers into the cart shed to take down the press gang.

Jamie says: "I thought to see your daughter home safely."

Scarlett's father brings his cup to his lips. "You and my daughter are not a good match. Leave her be. Leave my family be."

"I know what your family is."

"Then you'll understand it's not personal when I ask you to stay away."

Staying away, Jamie is coming to realise, is proving far more difficult than he had anticipated. "Do you know where she is?"

The man sighs heavily. "Scarlett wants nothing to do with me, as you well know. I got no idea where she is." He leans forward, pinning Jamie with hard eyes. "Listen boy," he says, "my family is in enough trouble without them getting involved with people like you."

"Trouble? What kind of trouble?"

He snorts. "I'm not in the habit of sharing my problems with the preventative service."

Jamie nods, only half listening. He looks through the window of the tavern. The path winds up over the cliffs towards Talland.

And before the thought is properly formed, he is riding that path, higher and higher, towards that cluster of red roofs, towards that church on the hill.

He weaves his way down into Talland. At the bend in the road sits the village tavern. Mariner's Arms, says the wooden sign above the door. Jamie remembers the place from Scarlett's stories. He will ask here. Hope someone can point him in the right direction.

If Scarlett and her family are in trouble, he needs to know.

She wakes to the feeling that she is not alone.

"Scarlett?"

It is Jamie's voice, but this is not possible. Jamie has ridden back to Portreath. He had waited for her in Polperro and she had not come to say goodbye.

She reaches for him anyway. Finds his arm, solid and warm. A noise comes from the back of her throat. Solid and warm and real. She grips tighter.

"You came looking for me."

"Why does that surprise you?" His voice is low and gentle.

Why? Because she had not seen fit to say goodbye? Yes, but there is more. She had not expected to find Jamie at her bedside because she had walked into the trap he had laid for the Portreath smugglers. She had sat in his cottage with stolen coins in her bodice. She has made a life doing everything he is trying to put an end to.

But he is here. Making her heart and breath quicken, as they had done each time his body jolted against hers on the journey from Portreath. Her heart and her breath, it seems, have little regard for who he is and what she has done.

She pulls herself from the pillow, ignoring the ache in her head. She wraps her arms around his neck and pulls him close. His hands feel solid and wide against the side of her ribs.

"I'm so sorry this happened to you," he says.

What is there to say? What is there to be done?

Scarlett doesn't answer. She presses her cheek into his

shoulder, feeling the coarse thread of his coat.

"Your father," he says after a moment. "He's in Polperro. Did you know it?"

Scarlett lets out her breath. No, he can't be here. Not among all this lightless chaos. She can't manage Jacob being here too. She waits for the anger at her father for following her. But it doesn't come, as though the Wild knows there is no room for it here now.

"What can I do?" Jamie asks.

Scarlett hesitates. Everything that needs doing cannot be done by a man who has sworn an oath to the revenue service. Whichever of her brother's enemies has taken the children, he is deep in free trade. Deeply entrenched in a world Jamie cannot be privy to.

In spite of it, she wants him here.

There is Gabriel and Mary and Reuben and Jacob. This unyielding, inescapable sightlessness. But right now there is Jamie. His arms around her and his hot breath on her neck. She wants to reach through the dark and touch every line of him.

But he has already seen far too much of the unlawfulness in her.

"Leave," she says, forcing herself out of his arms. "That's what you need to do."

"What?" The bed shifts, but he doesn't stand. For a fleeting second, Scarlett is glad she can't see his face. His voice has hardened. "I thought you trusted me."

"It's not about trust."

"Then why?"

How does she say it? How does she make sense of it? She needs Jamie to leave, because if he stays he will see all the dishonest, deceitful things her family does. How long will it be before he comes to despise her?

She feels him stand. Hears his footsteps move across the floor.

"Is that truly what you want?" he asks.

Scarlett doesn't reply.

The floor creaks on the opposite side of the room.

She throws back the blanket and slides out of bed. Her nightshift is thin. Barely reaches past her knees. She feels exposed. Indecent.

Where is the shawl Flora had tossed over her yesterday?

She fumbles on the chair beside the bed until her fingers touch the soft wool. She knots it around her shoulders.

Across the room, she hears Jamie breathe.

There are no footfalls. He is not coming to her. He is letting her find him. She is grateful for it.

This time there is no wall, no stair rail to guide her. Walking through the room is like finding her way through space.

Her outstretched fingers find Jamie's chest. She presses her palm hard against him.

How must she look to him, she wonders, with her vacant, useless eyes swimming through the dark? She lowers her head so he can't see her face. Feels his palm against her cheek. His fingers are rough and warm.

"Look at me," he says.

And she does. Turns to face him, lifts her eyes to his. And in her mind she sees him, the sharp jaw, the messy waves of hair, eyes the colour of winter sea. The image of him takes the tension from her shoulders and replaces it with a gentle fluttering in her stomach.

She wants to stay here forever, with her hand pressed to his heart, feeling the rhythmic thud of his pulse beneath her fingers. Life against life.

"Tell me what's happened," he says. "Tell me everything."

And of course, she cannot stay here forever. She cannot, even for a moment, pretend the world is as it should be.

"My niece and nephew are missing," she tells him. "They've been taken by whoever attacked me."

She hears Jamie's sharp intake of breath. Feels him shift beneath her.

"I may know where to look."

OLD SILENCE

Flora hands her clothing, one piece at a time. She waits patiently as Scarlett navigates the chaos of invisible buttons and laces.

The thick woollen stockings are her own; Scarlett recognises the darning on the heels and toes, the ribboned garters her own. Both have been washed and smell of soap instead of sea.

The petticoats are unfamiliar, as are the soft woollen skirts. Her own clothes are bloodstained, she imagines. Sea-stained, mud-stained. Perhaps beyond repair.

The bodice feels strange beneath her fingers. Flora's hand covers her own, guiding the lacing from one eyelet to the next, until Scarlett is bound tightly into the stays.

"Will you pin my hair?" she asks. She is going nowhere but her own cottage, but she feels the need to make herself presentable. She can't be this sorry, bed-ridden thing any longer.

She feels a brush tug through the thick snarls of her hair.

Flora is careful to avoid the gash on the back of Scarlett's head. "I assume," she says, light in her voice, "you might eventually tell me who this man is who came to my door in a panic, desperate to find you."

Scarlett feels a small smile in the corner of her lips. And then she thinks of Jamie waiting for her in the bar downstairs, pacing unwittingly above the smuggling tunnel. What would Flora think if she knew she had let a riding officer wander through her inn? Scarlett trusts Jamie, yes, but she knows she cannot expect everyone else to.

And so she tells Flora only vague outlines of the story; a man she had met on her travels, the man who had accompanied her home.

Flora slides the last pin into Scarlett's hair. "I'm pleased for you."

Scarlett presses against her skirts to feel her empty garter. "My knife. Where is it?" It must have been with her when Will had brought her to the inn.

"What do you need a knife for?" asks Flora.

Scarlett knows it is foolish. But the thought of stepping sightless into the world is terrifying. She has grown accustomed to the feel of having a knife at her knee. Has grown accustomed to the security of it.

"Do you have it?" she presses.

After a moment, Flora says: "Yes. In the kitchen."

And Scarlett speaks in a voice that clearly says she does not want to be judged. "May I have it?"

And so this is morning, shrouded in darkness. She hears the sea, hears the sob of the gulls, hears wind bend the trees. The air is cool against her cheeks. It smells of salt and washed up weed.

Scarlett's steps are tentative, and she grips Jamie's arm

tightly. But she knows this road well, she realises, this path that winds up to her cottage from the Mariner's Arms. She begins to walk faster.

"This way," she says. "Past the bell house." She needs to get to Isaac. Tell him all Jamie had told her about the crying baby in the castle. She is suddenly hot with urgency. "My cottage," she says. "It's the one by the bend. With the red chimney. Do you see it?"

"Yes."

"Is anyone there?"

"There's a light in the window."

Her fingers knead his arm. "Please don't say anything to my brother about our father. He doesn't know Jacob is alive."

"Is it not a thing you ought to tell him?"

Scarlett says nothing. She wants to tell Isaac. Needs his help to shoulder the load. But it cannot be now. "He's too much to deal with," she tells Jamie. "He doesn't need to know a thing about Jacob while his children are missing."

"I'll not say a word."

A sudden thought seizes her. She runs her fingers down the front of Jamie's coat. "What are you wearing?"

"You mean, am I dressed as the enemy?" She hears a smile in his voice. "No."

"Good. Best you don't say anything about that either."

She knocks lightly on the cottage door.

"Scarlett?"

She is glad to hear Isaac's voice. "I wasn't sure you'd be here," she says. "I thought you'd be out looking."

"Only came back for a little sleep." She can hear the strain in his voice. Wishes she could take it away.

"This is Jamie," says Scarlett. "He has information."

"Information?" She hears Caroline come towards them.

"I passed the ruins of Restormel Castle yesterday," Jamie tells them. "There were men hiding inside. Men who fired at me." He pauses, as though suddenly hesitant. "They fired at me after I heard a baby crying."

Scarlett hears a sharp intake of breath from Caroline.

Isaac says: "I'll go to the Millers' for the horse."

He and Jamie leave, plunging the cottage into silence. Scarlett sits on the floor beside the hearth, hugging her knees to her chest. How desperately she wants to be out there with them.

A chair creaks noisily, reminding her she is not alone. Caroline doesn't speak.

It has always been this way between the two of them. There is no chatter. No small talk. When they are alone, there is little to do but be silent.

But things are different now. The disappearance of Gabriel and Mary is an ache in Scarlett's chest. She can barely imagine how it must feel for their mother. A part of her wants to throw her arms around Caroline and tell her everything will be all right. But this is not the way things are between them. This is not the way things have ever been.

"We'll find them," she says instead. "I know it."

Caroline doesn't speak at once. "I'm sorry," she says after a moment. "You shouldn't have been caught up in all of this."

"If it were Reuben's doing, he has as much against me as he does Isaac."

"You believe it was Reuben?"

Scarlett curls her fingers around her knees. "It makes sense. He found the ankers in the tunnel. Knew you were trying to escape."

Caroline doesn't reply. Scarlett hears her leap to her feet

and hurry across the room.

"Stay here," she says.

"Where are you going?"

"To fetch more wood. The fire's almost burned out." The door swings open, letting a blast of cold air into the house. It slams heavily, a sound Scarlett feels in her chest.

She hears murmured voices. Who is Caroline speaking to? Scarlett cannot make out her words, but can tell she is angry.

The second voice comes again. A man's voice. It is faint, but familiar. Are her overworked senses playing tricks? Or is Asher Hales outside their house?

Scarlett stands. A hand out in front of her, she edges across the cottage. She clatters into the corner of the table, rattling the chairs. Pain shoots down her leg and she curses under her breath.

The voices stop abruptly.

"What are you doing?" Caroline demands, bringing another gust of wind inside with her.

"What are *you* doing?" Scarlett grips the edge of the table. She feels strangely unsteady, as though she were standing on a ship in the middle of a wild ocean.

"I told you, I was fetching more wood." Caroline locks the door and returns to the kitchen. Scarlett can tell there is no wood.

"Is Asher Hales outside?" she asks, trying to keep her voice even.

"Asher Hales? Of course not. What possible reason would he have to come here?" Without seeing Caroline's face, it is difficult to tell if she is lying.

Scarlett sits at the table. A log shifts noisily in the grate. "Asher told me to go to the cave," she says finally. "He told me you were hiding in there. I wasn't sure whether to trust him. I decided I had no choice." She touches the raw patches on her palms. She had torn the skin on the rocks when she had swum around the point to reach the landing beach.

"I've been telling you for weeks not to trust that man." Caroline's voice is cold.

"He couldn't have been the one who attacked you," says Scarlett. "He was on the cliffs with me."

"But he could have followed you into the cave. He could have taken the children."

"You believe it was him," says Scarlett. "You don't think it was Reuben. Why? Why would you suspect him?"

"Because I don't trust him."

"No. You never have. Why not?"

Caroline gives a cold laugh. "Do you truly need to ask that, Scarlett? You just said yourself, the man led you into the cave where you were attacked and blinded."

"Why have you never trusted him?" Scarlett hears her voice rise. The more Caroline speaks, the more certain she feels that it had been Asher outside the house. "Why did you have such hatred for him the minute I brought him through that door?"

"I suppose some people are just a better judge of character than others."

Scarlett clasps her hands together, tighter. She feels suddenly, intensely vulnerable. Caroline could come at her and she would have no thought of it.

She shakes the thought away. Foolishness. Surely this is nothing more than her racing, panicked imagination. Caroline is family. How many nights have they sat opposite each other at the supper table? Scarlett knows she would never hurt her.

But something has shifted. Intangible, but she can feel it. It as though something that has been in place for years has suddenly been dislodged.

"You don't need to be here," Isaac tells Jamie. He is riding a horse borrowed from a neighbouring farm. Climbs the steep hill a little too quickly. "I know how to find Restormel Castle. There's no need to put yourself in danger."

Jamie shakes his head. "There were men firing from the ruins. You ought not be there alone."

Isaac looks over his shoulder and gives him a short nod of thanks.

Up, up they wind. The path is narrow; trees on one side, sheer cliffs on the other. Isaac's eyes are fixed firmly on the brown mire of the road.

He has questions surely, about this man who had arrived on his doorstep with Scarlett's arm in his, claiming to know the whereabouts of his missing children. Jamie is glad he doesn't ask them. Scarlett has sworn him to secrecy on far too many issues. Best they ride in silence.

At last the hill peaks and an expanse of farmland stretches out before them. They goad the horses into a gallop. Jamie feels the vibration of hooves against earth deep inside his body. Wind stings his cheeks, sweeps the hair from his eyes. His ears burn with cold.

By afternoon, the castle is on the horizon; a dark shape in the shadows of the purple-green moorland.

They slide from the horses, tying their reins to the twisted trunk of the tree. Jamie feels that familiar edginess as they approach the ruins. He grips his pistol.

They enter through the main gate and weave through the

battered shell of the keep.

The ruins are silent. No footsteps, no gunshots. No cries of a child. The place smells of earth and old, cold stone.

Their footsteps echo. Neither of them speak, as though they are afraid shattering the stillness will cause the building to crumble. Shadows shift as the cloud bank thickens, making the muscles in Jamie's neck tighten.

Too quickly, they arrive back at the gate. They have circled the castle. Found nothing.

Isaac calls for his son. His voice disappears into the emptiness. He exhales sharply and leans back against the rugged wall.

Jamie looks sideways at him. There is plenty of Scarlett in him; the sharp coal-chunk eyes, the dark, unruly hair, the steely set of his jaw. Jamie has no trouble imaging this man sliding a shipment of liquor beneath the revenue men's noses.

He knows that had he looked at Isaac Bailey a week ago, he would have seen nothing but a thief. But perhaps the line between right and wrong is not always so clear. However entrenched in smuggling Scarlett and her brother are, they surely don't deserve to have their children taken or their sight stolen.

"I'm sorry," he tells Isaac. "They must have left after I caught them here."

"The man who was firing at you. You didn't see his face?"

"No. But there was something. So quick I can't be sure of it." Jamie hesitates. This doesn't feel the place for ghost stories. "Long dark hair. A man."

And Isaac begins to run, out through the ruins and across the plain towards the horses. Jamie charges after him.

"Where are you going?"

Isaac is breathless as he swings himself onto the horse. "I

know who's taken my children."

The old silence takes over.

Scarlett concentrates hard, trying to follow Caroline's every movement, trying to place her within the cottage. Her head begins to ache.

"Are you hungry?" Caroline asks finally.

Scarlett shakes her head. Her stomach is churning. Churning at the fear of Jamie and Isaac riding the moors. Churning at this new distrust of her sister-in-law.

"Here." Caroline pushes a glass into Scarlett's hand. She smells the hot tang of brandy.

"Are you trying to drug me?" she blurts.

Caroline doesn't speak at once. "I thought it might help you relax a little," she says. "God knows we could all use it."

Scarlett wraps her hands around the glass. Perhaps she is being foolish. Perhaps her imagination is racing in the dark and she is seeing danger where it does not exist.

She sips the brandy. Feels it slide warm down her throat. At the taste of it, she is back downing drinks after a run, back helping herself to the liquor kettle after a night's work at the Mariner's Arms. Things she fears she will never do again.

The silence is too much. Scarlett empties her glass and stands, feeling her way towards her bedroom. "Tell Isaac to fetch me," she says, "the minute he returns."

"I didn't expect you to keep me waiting," Asher says, when Caroline finally emerges from the house.

"What choice did I have?" Her voice is sharp and low. "Did you want Scarlett to hear everything?"

"Where is she?"

"Sleeping." Her eyes meet his.

Asher flinches under her scrutiny. The bruises on his face are yellowing, his hair stiff as straw. He had managed to find clean clothes at Leach's house, but the shirt is straining across his muscular shoulders and the sleeves of the coat dangle past his hands. There is little more degrading, Asher has realised, than wearing another man's clothes.

"Where are they?" Caroline's eyes are fierce, her voice wavering.

"I can't tell you that now."

She flies at him suddenly, her fists slamming into his chest. Asher's feet stay planted on the ground. He had been expecting such an attack.

A sob escapes her, and she covers her mouth. "You want Avery's money," she says finally.

"Of course."

Caroline blinks back her tears.

Asher feels something tighten in his chest. He could ease her sorrow, of course. Could take her to Polruan and show her where her children are lying, shoulder-to-shoulder on that pile of blankets Jane Leach had set up in front of the hearth.

He could make her happy, like he has always wanted to do.

He could do that, yes. But Asher knows he won't. It must be like this. Caroline has become manipulative, underhand. The only way to win is to play her game.

She shakes her head. "I don't know how to get to the money."

"Then I suggest you find a way."

She looks at the ground for a long time.

Asher feels nervous. Caroline is smart. She has trapped him before. He knows he must be on his guard around her. It was what had made him fall in love with her in the first place. She has always made him think. Challenged him. Never allowed him to become complacent.

But when she finally speaks, what she says is: "I will leave with you right now. Just take me to my children. And then we will go anywhere you choose." Resignation in her voice. "That's what you want, isn't it? To make a life with me, just as we used to talk about?"

Asher hesitates. He wants to leave this place with her, yes, but he needs Henry Avery's silver too badly to just walk away. "We can't have that life without the money," he says. "Without it we have nothing. What are we but paupers?"

"You will find another way to make the money you need," she says. "You're an intelligent man. The most intelligent I've ever known."

The words are heat inside him. Asher is dimly aware she is telling him only what he wants to hear. But he can't make himself care. Her praise tugs him back from the brink of self-hatred. Her praise reminds him of his great potential.

But he must not let himself fall for these honeyed words. "Why should I believe you?" he says. "You told me before you'd leave with me. And you led me into a trap. Threatened to frame me for the riding officers' murders."

"Why should you believe me?" Caroline repeats. "Because you have my children! Do you truly think I'd do anything to put them in danger?"

"I need the money," says Asher.

"And I need my children." Silence hangs between them.

Finally, Caroline asks: "Who attacked me? And Scarlett? I know it wasn't you. You're not capable of such a thing."

At the top of her cheek, Asher sees the angry red gash, the purple floret of bruising; evidence of Leach's attack. "I'm sorry. I never meant for you to be hurt." He hears his voice waver with a sudden rush of emotion.

Caroline presses her hand to his cheek. The unexpectedness of the gesture makes Asher's breath catch. At the feel of her skin against his, he is a young man again, overflowing with love and lust.

"Please," she says. "You loved me once. Perhaps you still do."

She is close to him, her breath hot against his nose and her fingers moving along his cheekbone. She is tugging the years away, taking him back to that ambitious man he used to be. How he wants to be that man again.

At the back of his mind, his common sense is roiling. She is playing him. This is love for her children, not love for him. But Asher wills that voice into silence.

She wraps her fingers around the laces of his shirt and pulls him towards her. Touches her lips to his.

And here comes his drive, his optimism, his dreams. Everything that had been sucked away by his conviction, his poverty, his shipwreck. Everything the Baileys had taken from him.

When Caroline pulls away, her eyes are glistening. "Take me to my children," she says. "And we will leave."

She is right. He is an intelligent man. He will find another way to make that money. And he will have Caroline by his side as he does so.

He nods slowly. "Get your things."

Caroline slips back into the cottage, leaving Asher waiting on the edge of the road. She creeps past Scarlett's door and into her own bedroom. Takes her cloak from the hook on the wall and slides it on. She feels strangely detached from her body. It has to be this way, she supposes. Let herself feel and she will crumble.

She runs a finger over the coarse thread of Isaac's pillow, swallowing the pain in her throat.

This will be the end. She will never lie in this bed beside her husband again. She will go with Asher Hales. There can be no more tricks or traps or manipulation. Not with her children's lives in danger. She will go with him as he wishes. And when his need for the money inevitably resurfaces, she will tell him all he wants to know.

Caroline's throat tightens. No, she will not cry. There is no time, no place for tears.

She pulls closed the door of her bedroom. Goes to the nursery. She has not been inside since her children were taken. She brings in no lamp or candle, unable to look too closely at its emptiness. But in the long, dusky shadows, she sees Gabriel's nightshirt, tossed on the floor in their desperation to escape Reuben's men. Toy soldiers are lined up on the floor by the foot of his bed, poised and silent. They have missed the battle.

What will the children need? They had been dressed for escape; Gabriel in his coat and scarf, Mary swathed in blankets. But she needs to take something for them, something that might help them feel close as she follows Asher away from her husband. Something to remind her that these sacrifices will be worth it.

She takes Gabriel's sap whistle and a rag doll for Mary. Stuffs them both into the pocket of her cloak and closes the door quickly.

Here is the reality she has been avoiding. She is to take them from their father.

She wishes she could tell herself she has no choice in the matter, but she knows it is not the case. She could disappear with Asher Hales and send Gabriel and Mary home.

But she cannot do it. If she is to vanish from this life, she cannot do it alone.

She will have her children and Isaac will have his pleasures at the inn on the hill.

She slips silently out the front door. She has left no note, no explanation. Let Isaac wonder, guessing at irreconcilable anger and secret love affairs. Nothing he imagines will be worse than the truth. He can never know she was the one who had forced his father to abandon his family.

Asher has a horse waiting, its reins looped to a tree close to the cottage. "Where are your things?" he asks.

"I have all I need," says Caroline. She has brought nothing but the toys and the clothes she is wearing. Why? Taking her things will raise Isaac's suspicions, of course. Does she want to be far away before he discovers she is gone? Prevent him from coming after her? Or it is more that this does not yet feel real? She will need no more than the clothes on her back because tonight, she will be home in her cottage.

Asher gestures to the horse. "I'm sorry. I've only one. We'll have to ride together." He does not sound sorry.

He offers his hand to help her mount, but she turns away and swings herself into the saddle. It has been many years since she has ridden, and she grips the pommel with white knuckles.

"You never used to ride astride," says Asher. He smiles close to her ear. "When did you stop caring about decency?"

Caroline bites back her retort. Asher Hales cannot see her animosity towards him. He needs to believe their love can be rekindled. Her children's safety depends on it.

The afternoon is grey as they ride the hill out of Talland. Rain spills over the cliffs, turning the dark ribbon of the road to mud.

Caroline can feel the heat of Asher's body. The nearness of him is uncomfortably familiar.

She wants to hate him. And a big part of her does. But she knows, of course, that she is not without blame. For years she has feared the repercussions of the things she has done. She has always taught her son to take responsibility for his actions. And she will do the same. To walk away from her life like this is the punishment she deserves.

Dusk turns the sea and sky purple. Wind cuts through Caroline's wet clothes, making her shiver violently.

They wind their way down into a tiny lamplit village. The river stretches out beneath them, silvery in the half light.

Asher stops the horse outside a small cottage behind the blockhouse. The walls are made of mismatched stone, the roof missing several tiles. One window is patched with a piece of colourless cloth.

Asher slides from the horse and offers a hand to Caroline. She leaps out of the saddle and charges towards the door.

"Whose house is this?" She peers through the grimy window. Can make out little but inky shapes inside.

"You don't need to know." Asher loops the reins to a nearby trough. He knocks on the door. "Jane," he calls, his voice low. "Let me in."

"Who is Jane?" Caroline hisses. "Who has my children?"

There is no response. Not from Asher, not from inside the house. Caroline pounds on the door again. "Who owns this house?" she demands. "Who are you working with? Tell me!"

Asher looks away. "Tom Leach."

"No," Caroline coughs. "No. Please tell me you're lying." Dizziness swings over her and she hunches, trying to gulp down her breath. She tears at the rag covering the window. Reaches through the jagged glass beneath it until her fingers touch the door latch. She pulls it open and races into the house. "Gabriel?" she calls. "Gabriel, are you here? Mary?" She charges through the cottage. Finds nothing but dark spaces.

A light flares in the kitchen.

Asher has a lamp in his hand, its flickering glow falling on a pile of rumpled blankets by the hearth. "They were here," he says.

Caroline reaches down and presses her fingers to the blankets. She feels her throat tighten, the whistle and rag doll heavy in her pocket. She sinks to her knees. She clutches at the blankets, trying to catch hold of any scrap of her children; a fragment of their warmth, a waft of their scent, a stray strand of hair.

"I'm sorry." Asher's voice is cracked. "Leach and his wife have taken them."

REPRIEVE

Caroline sits on the floor of Tom Leach's kitchen, holding her knees to her chest. Beside her, the logs in the grate are cold and black. Rain splatters against the glass. The flame in the lantern spits and vanishes.

Her feelings for Asher creep a little closer to hatred. But she cannot let herself feel it entirely. Hate him and she will be alone in this.

She ought to have known better than to trust Asher Hales to keep his word. This man has never been anything more than talk.

In the faint glow of the street lamp she sees him staring into the grate. He has knotted the laces of his shirt around one of finger.

"What does Leach want?" Her voice rattles. "The money?"

"Leach doesn't know about the money," he says distantly. "He just wants to punish your husband."

"Punish him? For what?"

"For turning him over to the authorities for murder."

"What?" Caroline cries. "That was not my husband's doing. It was Flora Kelly's." Rage flares inside her, hot and fierce. She cannot feel hate for Asher, Caroline realises, but she can damn well feel it for Flora.

She hears horses approaching the house. She leaps to her feet and peers through the window. There is Isaac, trailed by the man Scarlett had brought home.

Why are they here? She cannot make sense of it. But she doesn't care. She had never thought she would see her husband again.

She races out the door and throws her arms around his neck. For a fleeting second, that image of he and Flora together is gone. None of it matters. She just needs him close. His arms slide around her waist. And for a moment, Caroline lets herself breathe.

He steps back. "Why are you here?" He looks at her, then at Asher, who has stumbled into the street, unsteady as a drunkard. "Why are you with *him*?" Isaac lurches forward in anger, but Caroline grips his arms, holding him back.

"Mr Hales came to the cottage after you and Jamie left. Said he had information. He told me Leach had the children. But they're not here."

Isaac looks distrustfully at Asher. "How did you know it was Leach?"

"I saw him do it. I was on the cliffs at the time. I saw him go into the cave."

Caroline feels Isaac's arms tense beneath her fingers.

"You saw him take our children? Attack my wife and sister? And you didn't do a thing to stop it?"

Asher shrugs. "I was on the cliffs. There was nothing I could have done."

Isaac grabs the collar of Asher's shirt and shoves him hard

against the wall.

"Isaac, please." Caroline tries to force her way between the two men. "Stop." She plants a firm hand to her husband's chest. Feels his heart thundering. "Stop."

Isaac glares at Asher. "Why did you only think to tell us this now?"

Asher snorts. "Because I suspected I'd get a response such as this one."

Caroline turns to Isaac. "You knew it was Leach. How?"

He doesn't take his eyes from Asher. "Jamie saw him at the castle."

Caroline glances at Jamie; this tangled-haired boy who had appeared on their doorstep. The sight of him makes her think of Scarlett alone in the cottage. Alone in the cottage with far too many things to ponder.

Perhaps Scarlett could be convinced that it had not been Asher outside the door that afternoon. But it doesn't change the most brutal of facts. Scarlett knows her father is alive. And it will only be a matter of time before she tells Isaac.

If she hasn't done so already.

But Scarlett, for now, is a concern Caroline does not have room for. What Isaac's sister knows is inconsequential, as long as the children are in danger.

"Scarlett's alone at the cottage," she says, her hand still pressed against Isaac's chest. "Someone ought to go and check on her."

She feels a faint stab of guilt at having left Scarlett alone. But what choice had she had?

"I'll go back for her," Jamie says, his eyes darting towards Isaac as though seeking permission.

Isaac nods wordlessly. He watches Jamie leave, then swings himself onto his horse. "I'm going to the harbour to look for Leach's cutter."

Caroline nods. "I'll follow you. But I need to tidy the place first. I don't want anyone knowing we were here."

She stands in the doorway, watching the horse disappear around the corner.

Asher steps past her into the house. "I was wrong about you. You've become quite a liar."

Caroline turns away uncomfortably. She pulls the rag back down over the broken window and winds the edge of the fabric over the nails it had been attached to. "Tell Leach about the money. Tell him I know how to get to it. He can have it in exchange for my children's safe return."

Asher's lip curls. "That money is for you and I." He fades out as he speaks, as though he is coming to realise his worthlessness. He looks out the window into the dark street. There is little to see but a faint circle of lamplight. "I don't know where Leach is," he says finally.

"Find him."

He takes a step towards her. "If I tell Leach you know how to find the money, all your secrets will come out. It will destroy your marriage."

Caroline looks away. Asher is right of course. Jacob Bailey had been the one to tell her of the haul. And if she speaks of what she knows, the truth of all she had done to Jacob will spill out with it. But she has no choice. Her children cannot die to keep her secrets.

"Find him," she says again. "Please." She marches towards the door, desperate to go after Isaac. What would she have done, she finds herself wondering, had Asher led her to the children tonight? Would she truly have ridden out of her husband's life? Taken his children away without him ever knowing they were safe? Would she have had it in her? Even

Jacob had had the chance to say goodbye.

Asher snatches her arm. "Where are you going?"

"I'm going to find my husband."

His eyes flash. "You are to leave with me. We had an agreement."

She gives an incredulous laugh. "An agreement? An agreement is worthless if you cannot keep your word!" She yanks out of his grip. "You were unable to bring my children to me. You are full of lies, just as you have always been."

She sees the tremor of anger in his jaw. "That is not true," he hisses.

"Then prove me wrong. Find Leach. Tell him about the money. And get my children back."

A faint thread of moonlight makes the river shine. Beneath the dark water of the anchorage lies Leach's old cutter. Isaac had sent it there himself. But there is no sign of Leach's new ship. He is not surprised.

He sits atop the horse, feeling the animal breathe beneath him.

He has a name, at least. Knows which of these bastards they are looking for. But the thought brings little comfort. How can it when his children's lives are in the hands of a man with no morals?

He turns at the sound of footsteps. Caroline is trudging towards the harbour, her arms wrapped around herself and her shoulders drooped. The hem of her skirts is dark with mud. The weariness Isaac feels is etched in her face.

"His ship's not here," he tells her.

She nods, coming to stand beside the horse. She takes a rag doll from her pocket and runs a finger over its tattered face.

"I'll take the lugger out at first light," he tells her. "Search the coast."

Tears spill suddenly down her cheeks. She wipes them away with her palm.

Isaac reaches down and tentatively brushes the hair from her eyes. "Let's go home. There's no point us staying here. He's not coming back."

For a moment, Caroline doesn't speak. Finally, she nods and lets him pull her into the saddle. Her body sinks wearily against his.

He keeps his arms tight around her as they climb the hill out of the village. The rain has eased, but the roads are still slippery. He is careful not to push the horse.

Caroline's body is heavy against his. He presses his head into the crook of her neck. Every inch of her is achingly familiar; the strand of hair by her ear that never stays tucked beneath her bonnet, the coarseness of her damp cloak, her faint musky scent. That familiarity is an anchor.

"Please forgive me," he says, his words muffled by her hair. "What happened with Flora... it was a mistake. My loyalty ought to have been to you and the children. And I promise now it will be. Always."

At the mention of Flora, he feels her stiffen. But after a moment she sinks back into him. Covers his hand with hers.

A reprieve, Isaac thinks. A tiny flicker of optimism that he has not destroyed things between them forever.

He can't do this alone. Can't carry the weight of this. He knows Caroline can't either. They need each other.

"We'll be gone from this place soon," he says finally. "You and I and the children. I swear it." He presses a kiss into the cold skin on her neck. Can feel her trembling.

"I'm so afraid that will never be." Caroline's voice is distant and broken. Isaac feels it twist inside him.

"It will," he says. "We're going to find them. We have to believe that."

Caroline is silent for a long time. She leans into him, digs her fingers into his arm, gripping a fistful of his coat as though she were afraid to let him go. Then suddenly, sharply, she shuffles forward in the saddle.

"Do you love her?" she asks.

Isaac lets out his breath. "Caroline—"

"Just tell me." Her back is rigid, her eyes fixed on the road in front of them.

"You're my wife," he says. "That's all that matters."

Scarlett wakes from a sleep she had not intended to fall into. The world around her feels distorted. This is not the inn.

She panics, thrashes on her sleeping pallet. Her bed, she realises. She had fallen asleep here waiting for Isaac and Jamie to return. The thought calms her a little.

Around her, the silence is thick.

"Caroline?" Her voice disappears into the stillness. She is alone.

Outside, an owl coos. Night. How many hours has she slept? How long until morning?

What does it matter? Morning or night, the light is not coming.

She runs a hand along the side of her sleeping pallet, along the bedside table, over the cold stump of the candlestick.

Slowly, the familiarity of the room returns to her.

She had been alone in the darkness like this the day her mother had died. She had woken in the night to find her mother's raspy breathing silenced. Had gone to the room beside her own and found her staring motionless at the ceiling. Her chest did not rise or fall. Her fingers did not twitch. The illness she had promised would be a passing thing had claimed her in the night.

Scarlett had been five years old. She had crawled beneath her parents' bed and curled up in the dark. The light would come, she had thought. The light would come and make that chest rise and those fingers twitch. But when the light had come, it had shown every line and shadow on the colourless face that had once been her mother. Scarlett had run from the cottage on unsteady legs and belted on the door of her neighbour, Martha Francis.

And from out of the dark comes another memory. Her father bending over her bed, before the sun had risen. A kiss on her forehead, his cheeks wet. He had disappeared that day, and the village had believed him drowned.

He had known then that he would not be returning to Talland. Had believed he would never see her again.

She had forgotten those tears, that gentle kiss. Tears, surely, of man who had not wanted to leave.

A knock at the door.

"Scarlett?" It is Jamie's voice. She climbs hurriedly out of bed and makes her way across the cottage, traversing the gauntlet of chairs and tables and fire screens. She pulls open the door. The feel of Jamie's hands on her shoulders is steadying. The darkness feels easier to navigate.

"What's happened?" she asks. "Where are the children? Where's Caroline?"

The news is sickening. Tom Leach, says Jamie. Taken the children in an act of retaliation.

Scarlett lets out her breath. She had hoped for it to be Reuben. He at least operates under the illusion of decency. She sinks to the floor, hopelessness welling inside her.

So Leach was the one who had attacked her. The man who had cornered her in the cave and condemned her to this eternal dark. The Wild is there at her edges, threatening to tear itself free. And then Jamie sits beside her, sliding an arm around her shoulder and pulling her close.

Concentrate on the feel of him, she thinks. Concentrate on that warmth, on the pressure of his fingers against her arm. Concentrate on the smell of him; that faint scent of musk soap and horses and salty air. She breathes long and deep until the anger begins to fade.

She hears herself ask: "Where is my father?"

"At the inn in Polperro. Do you wish to see him? I think he would be glad of it."

Scarlett remembers herself suddenly. "No," she says. "I don't wish to see him. I want him gone from this place. If you see him, tell him to go back to Portreath." But a hint of regret lingers inside her.

What can I do, Jacob had asked, as she had stood in his cottage on the hill in Portreath.

Come back to Talland, she had said. Come back to Talland and save us from this life.

And here is he is.

She shakes the thoughts of her father away. There is no room for him in her head. No room for him in her life.

Suddenly she wants nothing more than to be out of this cottage where memories hang so thick in the air. She climbs to her feet and reaches for Jamie's arm. "Will you take me back to the inn?"

LOCKED DOORS

"Crowfoot," Flora tells Scarlett. "For illnesses of the eyes."

Flora has learnt to speak with confidence when she proffers cures to the other villagers. But today she can manage nothing more than thin uncertainty.

She is sure Scarlett sees the flaws in this soft-spoken attempt at a cure. She knows her blindness has been caused by a blow to the head and not an illness of the eyes.

But Scarlett says: "A cure?" There is too much hope in her voice.

Flora's stomach shifts uncomfortably. She takes Scarlett's arm and leads her to the bed.

Scarlett leans back, shifting the pillows beneath her to ease the pressure on the back of her head. Flora soaks a cloth in the water seeped with crowfoot. She wrings it out and places it gently over Scarlett's closed eyes. Water runs down her cheeks, leaving damp circles on the sheets.

Scarlett shifts suddenly, slightly. "What was that sound?"

The inn must be a warren of noises for her heightened hearing. As it changes shape with the weather, the Mariner's Arms rattles and groans like a ship at sea.

"It's an old place," says Flora. "The noises used to scare me as a girl." She allows herself a faint smile. "Sometimes they scare me still."

Scarlett brings a hand to her face, her fingers working across the damp cloth. "You must open your doors again," she says. "I'll not have you lose business because of me."

Flora sighs. "I'll not get by serving second-rate lambswool. And I can't risk selling liquor without a licence again."

"Plenty of taverns manage to survive as alehouses," says Scarlett.

"If they're taking storage money from smugglers on the side." Flora smiles wryly. "Perhaps I ought to have asked Reuben for a cut in exchange for his men using the tunnel."

There is no chance of such a thing now, of course. Whatever trust had existed between she and Charles Reuben had vanished the moment he had found Isaac's brandy ankers in the tunnel. "The only way I'll survive is to put guests up here."

"Would that be so bad?"

Flora doesn't answer. The more she thinks of it, the less she likes the idea. After all that has happened these past weeks, she has little faith in the goodness of strangers. "It's no matter," she says. "I can't find the key for the last room. I couldn't open it even if I wanted to." Carefully, she lifts the cloth. Scarlett keeps her eyes closed for a moment, as though afraid to open them. Flora's heart thuds. She needs this to work almost as badly as Scarlett does.

But when Scarlett opens her eyes, she lets out a heavy sigh. Her jaw trembles and she screws her eyes closed again, as though desperate not to let her tears escape.

Flora presses a hand over hers and squeezes. "Be patient. It may work yet." She is telling herself as much as she is Scarlett, she realises. There is a sick feeling in the pit of her stomach.

Scarlett sits abruptly. "Where are my boots?"

Flora gathers them from the floor and hands them to her. "Where are you going?"

Scarlett pulls them on, tying the laces with violent, angry movements. "I don't know. But I can't just sit around all day and hope." She climbs from the bed. "The keys," she says suddenly. "Can I try them?"

"If you wish."

Flora goes to the parlour for the keyring. She hands it to Scarlett, leading her down the passage towards the door of the third guestroom.

Scarlett presses an ear to the keyhole. "There's mice in there."

"I'm not surprised. It's been locked up since I was a child."

Scarlett begins to try the keys, shoving each one forcefully into the lock. The door will not open, Flora is sure. She has tried each of the keys at least three times.

She makes her way back towards the bedroom. Best she get rid of the crowfoot. Best not leave the scent to linger, reminding Scarlett of its failure.

She turns at a sudden thud. Sees Scarlett ramming her shoulder against the locked door. As Flora opens her mouth to speak, Scarlett kicks hard, the door flying open and pieces of the lock splattering over the floor.

"I'm sorry," she says, not sounding sorry in the slightest.

Flora hurries towards the room. The wood around the lock is splintered and rotting. Inside is dark, thick wooden blinds closed across the window. It smells musty and old. Forgotten.

Flora pulls back the threadbare curtains. The windows beneath are thick with grime. Little of the pale daylight makes its way through. She goes to the parlour and returns with the lamp.

"What's in here?" Scarlett asks.

The floor creaks loudly beneath Flora's boots. She had expected the room to be filled with her father's things. Locked chests and overflowing wardrobes, like she had found in the other two guestrooms. But there is no furniture here. Nothing but empty shadows. A threadbare rug is nailed to the floor. A mouse darts past Flora's boots and vanishes into a hole in the corner of the room.

She trails a hand along the wall. Feels a faint indentation beneath her fingers. She holds up the lamp.

Letters have been carved into the stone with a rough hand. They are arranged in a square, spelling unintelligible words. Flora has seen this arrangement of letters before. Her mother had written it on parchment to hang around her patients' necks. A charm against evil. A spell for the light.

She shivers violently, wrapping her arms around herself. The room is bitterly cold. Its unexpected emptiness makes her feel unsettled, as though she has spent her life living in a place she had not known at all.

"Flora?" Scarlett pushes. "What do you see?"

Lying on its side behind the door, she notices a small glass bottle, its contents dried and brown. She grabs it from the floor and slides it into her pocket. Makes her way into the hallway, ushering Scarlett out ahead of her. "Nothing," she says. "It's empty."

THE DEMONS OF BRIDLES LANE

In the afternoon, Flora feels herself drawn back to the third guestroom. She runs her fingers across the letters carved into the wall. Had her mother done this?

She pulls out the bottle and looks at it again. She has kept it in her pocket all day. It feels the safest place for it.

Dried blood inside, she is sure.

This arrangement of letters, this bottle of blood, Flora knows them charms against black magic. Charms to keep demons and dark spirits away from the living. Her mother had always believed such things necessary. She had sworn by her scrawled incantations, her witch bottles and watch balls. Had distributed charms for luck to the villagers each spring.

But there is something about these hastily scrawled letters that sends a chill through Flora's body. They speak of fear, of desperation. What had frightened her mother enough to take a knife to the wall of the house? Was it the reason she had locked the room up?

It doesn't matter, Flora tells herself. Her mother is at rest. She has been lying in her grave for more than three years. Whatever had frightened her is long gone.

But somehow it does matter. It matters because the thought of her mother in terror is one Flora cannot bear. And it matters because the Mariner's Arms is home. And if her mother had seen something within its walls that had scared her enough to barricade one of the rooms, Flora needs to know of it. In case whatever had scared her is not long gone.

She glances out the window. The sun is setting, and the sky is orange. People are filing out of the church. Flora squints. A baptism, perhaps. Yes, she remembers. The Millers' new baby. She had given skullcap to the midwife.

The vicar stands by the gate in his black robes, clasping the hands of his parishioners as they leave.

Impulsively, Flora grabs her cloak.

Bessie chases her down the stairs, her dog at her heels. "Where are you going, Mammik? Can I come?" She is out the door before Flora can respond.

By the time they reach the church, Reverend Dodge has returned to the vestry. Flora stands outside, watching Bessie tear across the grass with the dog. She feels strangely reluctant to enter.

At the sight of her, Dodge appears in the doorway. A smug smile turns his lips. He looks as though he has been waiting for this moment. Waiting for the witch from the inn to come to him, begging for him to cleanse her soul.

"Mrs Kelly," he says. "I'm glad to see you here." He gestures for her to enter. "You can come in, I assure you. The Lord will not strike you down." He laughs thinly.

Flora does not.

She steps inside, suddenly cold. The last time she had been

in the churchyard, she had watched George Gibson leap to his death. The last time she had been in the churchyard, she had watched figures move in the darkness. Seen things she does not believe in.

She looks up at the angular ceiling, looks at the coloured light straining through the windows above the altar. She hears Bessie call for the dog.

"Is something troubling you?" Dodge asks.

Flora hesitates. For a moment, she considers leaving.

Forgive me Father, this was all a mistake...

But she says: "I opened one of my guestrooms. And I found things in there that... unnerved me. There was an arrangement of letters carved into the wall. An arrangement my mother used to banish dark spirits."

Dodge hums.

"You know something of it," says Flora.

"Perhaps. Your mother called me to the inn many years ago. Back when you were just a child. She asked for my help cleansing the place. Exorcising it, as it were. I did as she asked, but it did not satisfy her. She asked me to return to the room and bless it on many occasions."

No. This is all far too familiar. She will not be drawn into another conversation with the vicar about the ghosts walking among them.

But she finds herself asking: "What did my mother believe she saw?"

"Demons," Dodge says plainly. "I told her she could expect little else, given her forays into black magic."

"Black magic," Flora hisses. "Please, Father, this is most offensive. My mother was just a healer, as you well know. She only ever did the things she did to try and help people." Anger bubbles beneath her skin. How foolish she has been to look to

103

Dodge for help. She ought to have known he would come back to her with *demons* and *black magic.*

He smooths his dark robes. "You came to me for answers, Mrs Kelly. I'm simply doing my best to provide them."

Flora grits her teeth. Could there be an inch of truth to the vicar's words? Though she does not believe demons walk the halls of the Mariner's Arms, she knows well her mother may have. But black magic? Surely not. Her mother had been a good woman. Had turned to charms and incantations to find cures, to lift curses. She had never been one to lay them. Dodge suggesting she had involved herself in harmful black magic feels like the greatest of insults.

Flora heaves open the door of the church. Bessie is picking at the ferns by the fence, close to where Flora had once seen a shape move in the shadows. The dog is weaving between the headstones, nose to the ground.

As she makes to leave, Dodge says: "Scarlett Bailey. How is she faring?"

"As well as can be expected. I'm doing all I can."

Dodge murmurs in response. "I worry for that girl. She has always been troubled." He runs a finger along the top of a pew. "It is hardly surprising, I suppose. Her parents didn't see fit to baptise her until she was more than a year old."

Yes, Flora has heard this. Two of Scarlett's siblings had gone to their graves days after their baptisms. An omen, of course. An omen of the worst kind. Jacob Bailey and his wife had not brought their youngest child before the vicar until she had seen out the deadly first year.

Flora feels a flicker of anger on Scarlett's behalf. "Jacob Bailey was very superstitious," she tells Dodge. "But that doesn't mean his daughter is troubled."

Dodge gives her a look that clearly tells her he is tired of her dissent. Who is this witch to step inside his church and question him? Fall into line or be swept up by the devil.

"She will be in my prayers," he says.

Flora regrets coming. "Thank you for your help," she tells him stiffly.

Dodge smiles without warmth. "I hope we will see you here on Sunday."

She gives a short nod and makes her way across the churchyard, her boots sinking into the damp earth. It feels as though the ground is trying to swallow her alive.

There, by the edge of the path is her mother's grave. A withered bunch of heather sits against the headstone. She ought to replace it. But she feels Dodge's eyes burning into the back of her. She calls for Bessie and hurries through the gate.

UNGODLY THINGS

It is past midnight when Isaac brings the lugger back into Polperro harbour.

The revenue men are waiting. Customs officers board the ship, raking through the hold in search of hidden contraband.

Isaac is in no mood for the interrogation. He has spent almost twenty-four hours searching the coast with Jamie and Will Francis. They are exhausted, frustrated. Have found no sign of Leach's black ship.

Isaac is not surprised by the revenue men's attentions. They have had their eyes firmly fixed on the place for weeks; desperate to find the scrap of evidence that might take down the Talland trading ring.

After a painfully slow and thorough search, the officers climb back to the deck. One gives Isaac a curt, wordless nod. The other two climb back to the harbour without so much as glancing at him. Their frustration at finding an empty hold is poorly hidden.

Will stares after the revenue men as they march back towards Customs House. "We'll go out looking again in the morning," he says. "First thing."

Isaac gives a nod of thanks to the two men. He is grateful for their selflessness.

He knows little of this man Scarlett had brought back to Talland with her. The few attempts Isaac had made at conversation with Jamie had been met with tight-lipped, insubstantial answers. Isaac hadn't pushed the issue. He'd not been in the mood for speaking either.

"Go home," he tells them. "Get a little sleep."

Will nods. "You ought to do the same."

Isaac watches the men leave; Jamie to the Three Pilchards and Will over the cliff towards Talland. He checks the moorings, then climbs from the ship and begins to walk towards the cliff path.

He hears footsteps behind him. Turns to see Reuben approaching the dock.

"I was beginning to think my ship had been stolen."

Isaac keeps walking.

"I require your services," Reuben says, keeping pace beside him. "I've word an East India merchant will be sitting at anchor outside the mouth of the river tomorrow night. A shipment of cognac and Burgundy wine. I've arranged for a purchase to be made."

"Go to hell," Isaac spits. "My children are missing. I'm not trading for you."

"Has there been any word of them?" Reuben asks dutifully.

Isaac grits his teeth. "Tom Leach has them."

"I see." Reuben's voice is calm and even, as though they

were speaking of the day's catch. "Then you will be searching the area around Polruan, I assume. Taking the lugger towards the Fowey river." Isaac catches the faint smile on the edge of his lips. "You'll meet the merchant, as I've arranged."

"And what will you do if I deny you? There's nothing more for you to take from me."

Reuben smiles thinly. "That is not entirely true, is it, Mr Bailey."

Isaac closes his eyes. Reuben is right of course. That bastard of a banker who acts on his superior's whim would not hesitate to hurt Scarlett or Caroline or Flora.

"Tomorrow night," says Reuben. "The mouth of the river."

Isaac quickens his pace. "I heard you the first time."

He sees little of the path in the faint moonlight. He is glad for the darkness. Concentrating on walking the cliffs stops his mind from straying to darker places.

From the top of the hill, he can see down into the village. A lamp is glowing in a window of the Mariner's Arms.

He doesn't mean to think of her. He knows how wrong it is for there to be anything in his mind other than his family. But she is there in his thoughts, where she has always been. The more he tries not to think of her, the more she fills his head.

Flora doesn't speak when she finds him on her doorstep. The green glass watch ball sways above her head as wind gusts through the open door. He pulls her into his arms. He needs the feel of her, the warmth of her. Needs her gentle voice, her intoxicating earth and brandy scent.

She pushes the door closed, without releasing her grip on him. Her fingers knot themselves in his hair. "What can I do?"

Isaac doesn't answer. *This. Just this.*

He wants to lose himself in that room at the top of the inn, wants to escape the nightmare his life has become. Wants to forget it all, never mind how fleetingly.

"You can't be here," Flora says, her voice low.

He knows this, of course. Knows that if anyone were to see them entwined like this, Flora would be shunned by the village for disregarding a man's marriage vows. And never mind the village, his sister is upstairs. Scarlett of all people can never know. He couldn't bear for her to discover he has betrayed his family like this.

And yet feeling Flora in his arms is the only thing that has slowed his heart in the four days his children have been gone.

He tries to take all of her in, running his hands over her arms, her hair, her skirts. She presses herself against him, as though willing to be taken.

He wants her lips, her skin, her ragged breath against his ear. But no. He cannot be this man. Cannot do this to Caroline.

Flora steps back. "You ought to leave, Isaac."

She is right, of course. And he hates that she is right.

He leaves without another word.

The Mariner's Arms has its shadows, but it has been many years since the place has stopped Flora from sleeping.

Perhaps it is not this empty guestroom that is causing her sleeplessness. Perhaps it is the ghost of himself that Isaac has left behind.

The inn is silent; Scarlett and Bessie sleeping. It must be close to dawn. Flora is glad when the dog scampers down the passage, the tapping of his claws breaking the stillness. He stops at the doorway of the guestroom. Flora crouches, calls to him. He stays planted in the doorway, ears pricked up and whiskers twitching.

She looks down at the rug nailed to the floor. It is worn through to its thin reed matting, with just a few sparse patches left of its original blue and green. Flora remembers her father arriving home from a merchant voyage with it rolled up on his shoulder. Remembers him unfurling it over the parlour floor, turquoise as a piece of the sea. She had spent hours crawling back and forth across it, entranced by the softness of it beneath her palms.

How has it ended up here, neglected and forgotten?

She grabs a corner and yanks hard, until the nail holding it to the floor flies free. Another corner, another, another until the rug lies curled up in the centre of the room.

There is something beneath it.

She pulls the rug away and crouches, holding the lamp close to the floorboards. A scratching in the wood. A faint circle, hemmed with carved symbols she cannot make out.

She knows this, like she knows the letters on the wall. A magic circle, for the conjuring of spirits. Her stomach lurches.

Her forays into black magic...

"No Mamm," Flora says, aloud. "What did you do?"

Black magic, her mother had taught her, was a dangerous, powerful thing. A thing never to be spoken of. A thing far too dangerous to go near. It had the power to end life, the power to change the past and future, the power to call up spirits.

Her mother had been terrified of demons and ghosts. As far as she was concerned, they were frightening, undeniable things woven into the fabric of life. What could have led her to dabble with such things?

Little wonder she had been scared enough to hack the

letters into the wall. Little wonder she had filled the bottle with drops of her own blood. Flora knows the enchantment. A drop of blood from the bewitched to set the darkness at rest.

Why does this bother her so, she wonders? She doesn't believe in such things. Why does she care that her mother had played at the edges of something ungodly?

It bothers her, she realises, because she has begun to shape her own life around the craft her mother had lived by. A craft she believed was intended to help, never to harm. What else had the village charmer seen fit to do? How much of her craft had she kept hidden from prying eyes?

And it bothers her the most that Dodge was right. Bothers her that the vicar had known more about the village healer and her craft than her own daughter had.

The rap of the brass knocker yanks Flora from her thoughts. She hurries downstairs, half hoping for Isaac, half hoping for anyone else.

She finds Caroline on her doorstep.

Flora feels a violent stab of guilt. There ought to have been apologies, a shamefaced explanation at the very least. In light of all that has happened, Flora had felt it best to stay away. But now such a thing feels like the greatest act of cowardice.

"I'm sorry," she says, before Caroline can speak. "I don't expect forgiveness. I just—"

"I'm not interested in your apologies. I need your help."

"My help?"

Caroline tugs her cloak tighter around her body. "Everyone says you have your mother's skills." The sharpness in her voice has been replaced with uncertainty.

Flora looks down. "I really don't—"

"Believe me, I wouldn't come to you if I weren't desperate. But Tom Leach has my children. I'm willing to try anything."

"Tom Leach?"

Scarlett had said nothing of this when she had returned to the inn last night. Nor had Isaac mentioned it when he had appeared on her doorstep earlier. No doubt they had both sought to protect Flora from her own guilt. Caroline clearly has no such sensibilities.

"He's taken them because he believes Isaac was the one who turned him over to the revenue men," she says pointedly.

"I'll go to him at once. I'll tell him it was me."

"And put your own child in danger?" Caroline's knuckles whiten around the hem of her cloak. "We've no idea where he is. Isaac has spent all day looking for him."

"I'm sorry," says Flora. "More than you could know."

Caroline looks up at the watch ball. "I've been in this place long enough to know the stories. Magic mirrors that show you hidden things."

Flora's stomach turns over.

"You have one."

She nods slightly.

"Could it show you where Tom Leach is hiding?"

Flora swallows. She doubts, of course. Doubts herself, doubts the mirror. But her uncertainty had not helped Scarlett and it will not help Caroline. Or her children.

She steps aside and gestures to the staircase. "Upstairs."

Flora perches on the edge of an armchair in the parlour, the black mirror across her lap. Caroline sits in the chair opposite, arms folded tightly, eyes fixed to the floor.

Flora tightens her grip on the handle of the mirror. How desperately she wants to be of use.

She had seen the murder of the riding officers in the glass, she reminds herself. Had seen dead men on the road, as clearly as if they had been lying on the floor beside her.

What had she been doing to bring about such a vision?

She closes her eyes momentarily, willing her thudding heart to still. She blinks, then lets her eyes relax as she stares into the dark surface.

She sees her own face, sees the dance of the candles behind her. But she needs more. Needs an image in the glass. A glimpse of Tom Leach, or the children, or anything that might begin to atone for the crime she committed when she took another woman's husband to her bed.

There is nothing to see but her own distorted reflection.

"I'm sorry," she mumbles. "I wish I could be of more use. I really do."

For a long time, Caroline says nothing. She stares into the fire, winding a stray strand of hair around her finger. "Did you pin her nightgown?" she asks distantly.

"What?"

"Bessie. Did you pin her nightgown to the crib? To stop the fairy folk from taking her?"

Flora reaches out and presses a hand to Caroline's wrist.

She pulls away sharply and leaps to her feet. "I don't know why I came. You can't help me." She turns and rushes down the stairs, disappearing into the dark tavern.

Caroline throws open the front door of the inn. What had she been thinking? She is not a woman who believes in magic.

She stops suddenly, looking over her shoulder into the empty bar. The key to the cellar is in the lock.

She lets the front door close heavily, then creeps towards it.

She lights the lamp at the top of the stairs and climbs down into the shadows. Broken chairs lie scattered over the cellar floor, ale ankers piled up in one corner. Larger barrels are stacked up against the wall.

Shoving one aside, Caroline sees she is standing at the mouth of the tunnel. The passage into the rock is smaller, tighter than she had expected. The sight of it is unsettling. She has never liked the idea of Isaac traipsing through the centre of the cliff. She likes it even less now she sees how narrow and black it is. An easy place, she thinks, for a man to die. She slides the barrel back into place.

Holding the lamp close, she runs a hand across the cellar wall. And she finds what she is looking for. Finds what Jacob Bailey had led her towards. An irregularity in the bricks.

Jacob had not been playing her. He had not been lying. Here is a place where the wall has been broken into. A place where the bricks have been removed, then carefully replaced.

A perfect hiding place for foreign silver.

A BLACK SHIP

Asher wakes from a broken sleep on the floor of Tom Leach's kitchen. It is still dark, but he feels as though he has slept several hours.

The door clicks open. "Mr Fielding? Are you there?" It is the voice of Jane Leach.

He scrambles to his feet. Jane is breathless and flushed, strands of red hair plastered to her freckled cheeks. Muddy skirts cling to her boots. "I couldn't stop him," she says, gulping down her breath. "He came in the morning, after you'd left. He believed you were planning to give them back to their mother. Said he couldn't let such a thing happen."

"Where are they?" Asher asks. "Did he—"

"They're alive," says Jane. "I begged him not to hurt them. I went with him because I was so afraid of what he might do."

"Where is he now?"

"He's on his ship. He thinks I'm sleeping. I managed to get out without him noticing." She winds the edge of her cloak

115

around her finger. "I can take you to where he's moored. But we've got to hurry."

Asher pulls on his coat and follows Jane out of the house. The dawn is pearly and purple, the streets glistening after a sprinkling of rain.

What is he doing? Why is he walking in the direction of Tom Leach? The man could kill him in a second. Is likely to do so if he discovers Asher has been to Caroline.

But there is something about those children that is pulling him towards them. Is it the fact that they have Caroline's blood running through them? Or is it his own regret at having done what he has? His last lingering scraps of decency?

Asher follows Jane up the hill out of the village. She leads him along the narrow path worn into the top of the cliffs. Her head is drooped, her shoulders hunched. She looks over her shoulder at him. "You don't seem like a man who would do such a thing."

And what do I seem like, Asher thinks to ask? What kind of man do I appear to be? If one was to glance at him, would they see any scrap of that life he so longs for? Is there even a ghost of that man left inside him? He is sickened by how far he has fallen.

He thinks of who he had been before he had returned to Cornwall. He had been the man who could see the beauty, the mysteries of the human form. The man one episode away from catching the soul in its escape from the body. One episode away from great scientific discovery.

Now he is a man whose dreams lie in pieces. A man who has taken the wrong path.

"It's gone too far," he admits, his voice low.

"Yes," Jane says dully. "When you involve yourself with Tom, this is usually the way things end up."

She gives him a wry smile that doesn't reach her eyes. She is older than Asher had first thought; past thirty, perhaps. Still far younger than her husband. A caring, gentle woman. How had she ended up sharing Tom Leach's bed?

"He was not always the way he is," she says, as though reading his thoughts. She watches her feet as she walks. "We had children of our own once. Three boys. Influenza took them all in a winter. Tom weren't the same after that."

Asher wraps his arms around himself to keep out the wind. "So he will kill another man's children to make up for his own loss?"

"No," says Jane. "He will kill another man's children to see his own sense of justice done."

"Down here," she says finally. The path veers down the rugged slope of the cliff. Asher plants a hand into the grassy bank to steady himself. His boots crunch into the pebbles at the bottom.

Leach's cutter sways on heaving grey water, its black masts barely visible between the folds of the cliff. Jane's boots crunch across the shore towards the dory she had left on the beach.

Asher shoves the boat into the water. It sighs noisily through the pebbles. He looks over his shoulder at Jane. "You could leave now," he tells her. "Be free of him. What life can he give you as a wanted man?"

She picks at the dirt beneath her fingernails. "No. He's my husband." More picking. More dirt. A swell of sea washes over her boots.

Asher feels a pang of curiosity. Had her husband held her as they had buried their children, he wonders? Had they wrapped themselves in each other's arms in an attempt to ease their grief? He finds it hard to imagine Tom Leach capable of such things. What does this woman see in him that is so meticulously hidden from the rest of the world?

Jane knots her skirts above her knees and wades through the water. She climbs into the dory, making it lurch wildly. Asher jumps in after her and begins to row.

He watches the beach grow distant. Can feel the cutter looming behind him. When the shadow of the ship falls over them, he lifts the oars and lets the dory drift. He reaches out a hand to stop the boat knocking against the hull. Above their heads, the cutter is quiet.

"You ought to go aboard first," he tells Jane. "Get back to your bunk before he notices you gone."

"The children are in hold," she whispers. "You've got to get them off the ship. I'll try and get Tom into the cabin so you can go in through the saloon." She reaches for the ladder and pulls herself onto the rungs.

Asher waits until she has disappeared over the gunwale, then uses the mooring rope to attach the dory to the ladder. He climbs onto the ship, feeling it sway with the tide.

The deck is still and dark. Ratlines clatter above his head as wind whips up the water. He pulls the hatch open a crack. Peers into the saloon. He sees no one. Murmured voices come from inside the cabin.

Asher hurries down the ladder and slips into the hold. It is dark, full of inky shapes. He waits on the ladder as his eyes adjust to the lightlessness. He cannot see the children.

Above his head, the voices grow louder. Leach has emerged from the cabin and is marching across the saloon.

"Did you go to the authorities then?" he demands. "Did you tell them where I'm hiding? Do you want to see your own husband on the scaffold?"

"No," Jane coughs. "Of course not. I didn't go anywhere."

Asher hears a thud, then her muffled cry of fear.

In the hold beneath him, the baby begins to shriek. Asher slides down the ladder into the dark, feeling his way between water kegs and lines. He sees Gabriel on his knees, crawling towards his sister.

Leach rips open the hatch, letting a stream of light into the hold. Asher darts forward and pulls Gabriel back into the shadows. He feels him trembling.

Jane pushes past Leach and scrambles down the ladder. "Let me take her," she says. "I'll calm her down." She grabs Mary from the floor, her eyes gliding over Asher and Gabriel. The baby held tightly to her chest, she makes her way out of the hold.

"How long are you planning on mothering these scraps for?" Leach demands.

Jane's response is fiery. "As long as I need to. I'll not let you harm them."

Asher releases his hold on the boy. "Can you row a dory?"

Gabriel nods.

"Good. The boat is tied to the bottom of the ladder. You've got to go. Now, while they're in the cabin. Follow the coast and it will take you back to Talland."

Gabriel's eyes are wide with fear. "What about Mary?"

"We'll not get her out now. Not without Leach seeing. You've got to go. Tell your parents where the ship is."

The boy shakes his head. "I have to get Mary."

Asher grits his teeth. "I will get her," he says sharply. "You've got to get off this ship. Or you're both going to die."

"No!" he hears Jane cry. "Please, Tom. You can't!"

Gabriel rushes towards the hatch. Asher grabs his arm, yanking him back. He scrambles out ahead of the boy. Leach is marching up the ladder to the deck, Mary tucked beneath his arm. She is shrieking. Jane is shrieking. Tears are flooding both their faces. Jane grabs her husband's arm, trying to pull him from the ladder.

"Please Tom!" she cries. "Please!"

Leach shakes her off.

Asher races up the ladder after them. Jane is a flurry of desperate hands, clutching at her husband's coat, trying to pull the baby from his grip. Leach pushes past her, making for the gunwale. For a moment, Asher's vision swims. There is the sea. And Caroline's daughter. The child will die, and it will be his fault. He will lose any hope he might have had of a life with the woman he loves.

"Don't," he says suddenly.

Leach whirls around in surprise.

"Her mother. She knows things. Knows how to find a fortune."

"What are you talking about? How did you find me?" Leach turns to glare at Jane. He shoves her away as she makes another desperate lurch for the baby.

"There's money hidden somewhere in Talland," says Asher. "And Caroline Bailey knows how to find it. But if you kill her daughter you'll have no way of bargaining with her."

He hears the faint creak of the hatch. He steps back, back again, trying to draw Leach across the ship. Trying to give Gabriel a chance to disappear behind them.

Leach takes a step towards him, the baby shrieking and thrashing beneath his arm. "Why should I believe this?"

"Is it not worth taking the risk that I might be lying?"

Behind Leach and Jane, Gabriel slips out of the hatch on soundless feet. He climbs over the gunwale and onto the ladder.

"A haul of silver," says Asher, "brought to Cornwall by Henry Avery."

"And how does Bailey's wife know about this?" Leach's eyes are distrusting, but Asher can see he has his attention. He shoves Mary back into Jane's arms and Asher lets himself breathe.

"Someone told her of it," he says. "Her father-in-law."

Out of the corner of his eye he sees the dory slide away from the ship and begin to move across the sea.

LOYALTIES

Scarlett wakes to the sound of footsteps in the room she had kicked open. It is early, she guesses. The air is cold, and the street quiet. The groan of the floorboards is all she can hear. She climbs out of bed and makes her way to the guestroom.

"Flora? Is that you?"

"Ayes. Are you all right?" Her voice is tired.

The musty smell is strong, though not as pungent as it had been the day before. Scarlett runs her hand along the wall, trying to see the room through her fingertips. It is cold inside. "Have you slept?" she asks Flora.

"Not really."

"What have you been doing?"

Flora sighs heavily. "Trying to use the mirror."

"The black mirror?" Scarlett kneels beside her. Her fingers move across the floor and brush the cold glass. "You've been trying to use this all night?"

122

"My mother used to say it worked best for her when she'd not slept."

"What do you hope to see? The children?"

Flora doesn't answer at once. "Caroline came to see me last night," she says finally.

Scarlett sits up. "What did she want? Did she say anything to you? About Asher Hales?"

"Asher Hales? No. She just asked for my help finding the children. But I wasn't able to give it."

There is a knock at the door. Flora climbs to her feet, her footsteps disappearing out of the room and down the stairs.

Scarlett stays kneeling on the floor. She lifts the glass, imagines herself looking into it. Images flow through her mind: sea, ships, her father. Just her imagination? Or can the dark glass penetrate her unseeing eyes?

"Scarlett—"

Flora's voice makes her start. She lowers the mirror, feeling foolish.

"Jamie is downstairs. He wishes to see you."

Scarlett leaps to her feet and hurries down into the bar.

"It's early," says Jamie. "I know. I just—"

"It's all right. I'm glad you're here."

"Your father came to me at the inn yesterday," he says. "Asking if I knew anything about the children. He's very worried for them. And for you."

Scarlett sighs heavily. She doesn't want Jacob here. It is only a matter of time before he crosses paths with Isaac. She is not sure her brother could handle walking past their dead father in the street.

"He doesn't have the right to worry for us," she tells Jamie. But she can hear the weariness in her voice. She is tired of anger. Tired of rage. Tired of the darkness that lies coiled inside her. How can she deal with the darkness within when she has nothing but darkness without?

"He wants to see you," says Jamie, his hand against her wrist. "Perhaps you might let him?"

And so it is to be like this. Lawful, decent Jamie is to play peacemaker between she and Jacob. She feels hot with frustration. Jamie knows well the things her father had been involved in. He had taken down his press gang himself. Why is he so eager for them to reconcile?

But she finds herself saying: "Tell him I will meet him on the beach."

"Is he there?" she asks. Her boots sink into the wet sand of the landing beach, a fine mist of sea cold against her cheeks.

"I'm here, Scarlett," Jacob says, before Jamie can answer. "What can I do?"

Leave, she thinks to say.

But something stops her. Is it the fact that Jacob is here, come to Talland as she had asked? Or is it the memory of his wet cheeks, as he had bent to kiss her goodbye?

No, she will not let herself be swayed by hazy recollections. Jacob Bailey is a murderer. He had taken down a man in the very place they are standing.

She had asked Jacob to meet her here on the landing beach, so he might be forced to remember the things he had done. But had she asked him to meet her here, so she might also not forget?

Why had she agreed to meet him in the first place?

"You can't do anything," she tells him. "There's nothing to be done."

"I want to help find whoever did this to you. And I want to help Isaac find his children."

"Isaac doesn't know you're alive."

"You've not told him." His voice is flat.

Scarlett says nothing.

"Why not?"

"Do you truly think he would care to know? After you disappeared and left him to pay your debts?"

Though she doesn't want to admit it, Scarlett knows there is also a part of her that wants to keep Jacob a secret. If Isaac were to know, the decision of whether to allow their father back into their lives would no longer be hers alone. She needs that control.

"I want to help," Jacob says firmly.

"It's too late for that. You made it clear a long time ago where your loyalties lie."

"My loyalties lie with you, Scarlett," he says. "They always have. I—"

"How can you say that? After all this? Everything that's happened to me, and to Isaac's children, it's all because of you! It's your fault we got caught up in this life! It's your fault we've had anything to do with Reuben or Tom Leach or this smuggling ring! I want nothing more to do with you. And I know Isaac would say the same." She turns abruptly, stumbling up the beach. Feels a hand around her arm.

"He wants to help you, Scarlett." Jamie speaks softly. "Let him."

Anger boils inside her. She yanks her arm away. "My father is a smuggler and a murderer, Jamie." Her voice is loud. She hopes Jacob can hear. "He was a part of the press gang who took your brother. He is everything you despise. Why do you have such trouble understanding that I don't want him in my life?"

"Just hear him out. You needn't do anything more."

She can't pretend to be surprised by his response. Decent, upstanding Jamie. He makes her feel like a terrible person.

She shoves hard against his chest. Feels him stumble backwards with the shock of it.

And she starts to run, her legs pumping, energised by the Wild. Beneath her feet, the path rises in the same narrow ribbon it has for her entire life. She hears the sea thrash and sigh against the rock. There is a strange thrill at knowing the earth could disappear from beneath her feet at any moment. It makes her feel alive.

She feels her hair lash against her cheeks, hears Jamie call after her. She keeps running. His footsteps, his shouting grows closer. And his arms are suddenly around her, squeezing her tightly, holding her still. She thrashes against him.

"Stop," he says breathlessly. "Stop. You'll fall."

Forced into stillness by his firm grip, she stops writhing and gulps down her breath. Her blood is hot. She can feel it thumping behind her eyes. The Wild is tangling her thoughts, making firecrackers of phantom light dance across her vision. She has little recollection of what she had said to her father.

How does she stop this anger? How does she free herself? The dark is all around her, powerless to take the Wild away. The dark has always brought her peace, but all she craves is the light.

She closes her eyes. It does nothing of course, but perhaps for a moment she can convince herself that the darkness is a choice. She lets herself fall into the great expanse of it. That endless void that steals her anger. Her heart begins to slow, and she sinks to the ground, suddenly exhausted. The damp earth soaks through her skirts. She brings her knees to her chest. The Wild has slunk away. But it is too late. Jamie has seen.

Tears spill down her cheeks. "I never wanted you to see this side of me."

She hears the long grass rustle as he sits. For a long time, he doesn't speak. Scarlett feels his hair tickle her cheek. A fine rain has begun to fall, and she lifts her face to the sky.

"Why does your father make you so angry?" he asks finally.

Scarlett grabs a fistful of his coat, needing him closer. "He left us," she says. "He left us to carry his debts. Left my mother to die of grief. Nothing he does can take that back." She turns to face the sea. Imagines it beneath her; grey and white and shifting. She takes a long breath, trying to find calm. "I wish you hadn't told him about the children," she says finally.

Jamie hesitates. "I didn't. He was the one who told me his family was in trouble. It was why I came back to Talland to look for you."

Scarlett frowns. "How else would he have known?"

"I don't know." Jamie squeezes her shoulder. "This is a small village. Word spreads. You know how things are."

"Are you sure you said nothing?"

"I'm certain."

Jamie leaps suddenly to his feet. He speaks fast, frantic.

A dory, he is saying, rowed by a child.

A child with dark hair? Yes.

"It's Gabriel," says Scarlett. "It must be." She feels Jamie yank on her hand as he begins to run down the path. She hurries after him.

The sea is rough, he tells her as they run. Gabriel will need help to land.

And in her mind's eye Scarlett sees that little boat lurch as the sea does its best to tear it away from their shore.

Jamie scrambles onto the rocks at the edge of the beach. The current has caught hold of the boat and is sweeping it past the narrow pocket of sand and shale. From here he can see around the point to a second crescent of rock-hemmed beach. The boat is see-sawing on the swell. He tears at the buttons of his jacket, then stops. Another figure is moving through the water. Scarlett's father. He has left his coat on the sand and is swimming towards the dory.

"What's happening?" Scarlett pushes.

"Your father," Jamie tells her. "He's swum out to the boat. He's helping Gabriel bring it in. They'll land on the beach around the point." He wonders if Jacob knows the boy is his grandson.

Jamie takes a step higher up the wall of rock. Behind the half-moon beach, the cliffs rise steep and dark. The only way back to the village is over the rocks and through the sea.

"Go to the cottage," Scarlett tells him. "Tell Isaac and Caroline that Gabriel is at the inn."

"The inn?" Jamie repeats. "What do you mean? He's landing on the beach."

"Don't ask questions," Scarlett says sharply. "Just get them."

"What about you?"

"I can find my way there."

"Are you sure?"

"Yes." Urgency in her voice. "Go. Quickly."

Jamie looks back over his shoulder. Sees the boy and the old man stumble up the beach and vanish into the cliff.

He goes to the cottage. Catches Isaac on the path, heading

for the harbour.

"The inn," he says. "Gabriel is at the inn."

"What?" Isaac doesn't wait for Jamie to respond. He returns to the cottage for his wife, then they are charging down the hill towards the tavern.

Jamie follows. Scarlett has made it to the inn and is thumping on the door.

"He came in on the dory," she tells her brother. "Made it to the eastern beach."

No mention of their father, Jamie notices.

Flora opens the door, a dog yapping around her ankles. Caroline pushes past her and opens the cellar door. As she does so, the boy stumbles out, his dark hair windswept and tangled. He lets out a choked cry and throws his arms around his mother.

"Mary," says Caroline, gripping his grimy cheeks in her hands. "Where's Mary?"

Gabriel sniffs. "She's still in the place. On the boat."

Jamie stands with his back to the wall. He feels an intruder. He hears Scarlett call his name.

"I'm here," he says, reaching for her arm.

She stands with her shoulder pressed to his. She is calm now; the rage drawn away. He is coming to recognise this about her; the way her moods rise and fall like sea. Still, he had not been prepared for the violent squall that had torn through her on the cliffs.

"Is he here?" she asks under her breath. "My father?"

"No."

Jacob has stayed hidden. Perhaps Scarlett's outburst on the beach has shown him such a thing is for the best.

Jamie glances at the open door of the cellar. And he finds himself walking towards it. Is he looking for Jacob? Or does he want to see what else is down there?

Perhaps a little of both.

He climbs down the stairs, squinting in the dark. Barrels are stacked up along the wall. Two are lying on their sides, as though they have been shoved out of place. Behind them, the rock gapes. His curiosity getting the better of him, he peers into the hole. He sees shoring timbers, and then darkness as the passage vanishes into the cliff.

He had known this, he reminds himself. He had known from the beginning what he was taking Scarlett home to. But the sight of the smuggling tunnel reminds him of all they have been unable to speak about. That bridge they are unable to cross.

What is he doing here in Talland? He has a comfortable home in Portreath, honourable work. Honourable work he is jeopardising each day he stays in this place. He had told his commanding officer he would be away no more than four days. Two days to Talland, two days back to Portreath. He had not counted on entangling himself in the nets of these smugglers.

But how can he leave? How can he ride away when Scarlett's world is falling down around her? Despite the smuggling tunnel and her light fingers and the pocket stitched on the inside of her cloak, she has made him feel things he has never felt before.

He is not sure he could ride away now, even if he wanted to.

He hears the stairs creak.

"Your father's not here," he says.

Scarlett nods slowly. She turns away, as though doing so might prevent him from seeing too much. Prevent him from seeing her shame. There is so much of her she doesn't want him to see, he realises.

She feels her way towards the mouth of the tunnel.

"Are you there?" she calls softly.

But there is silence. Nothing but the sea sighing distantly through the rock.

BRUTAL MEN

"The man from the wreck told me I had to leave without Mary." Gabriel's words are muffled against his mother's shoulder. "He said if I didn't we'd both die."

Caroline sits close to the fire with Gabriel in her lap, his long legs on either side of her and his arms curled around her neck.

Isaac crouches beside them. "You had to go," he says gently, a hand pressed to Gabriel's back. "You had no choice."

His son looks at him with tired and frightened eyes. Isaac takes a long breath. Does he feel violent relief that Gabriel is safe? Or terror at the thought of precious, uncomprehending Mary alone in the hands of Tom Leach? Uncomprehending, he supposes, is something of a blessing.

"Where is the man from the wreck now?" he asks Gabriel.

"I don't know. He just told me I had to leave."

"Tell me again," says Caroline. "Anything you remember.

Anything you saw when you got off the ship."

"I don't know. I only remember the sea. And the cliffs."

"Which cliffs, Gabriel?" Caroline pushes. "Where?"

"I don't know."

She rakes her hands through his tangled hair. "Please, my darling. You have to think harder."

Gabriel shakes his head violently. Buries his eyes in Caroline's neck.

Isaac touches her shoulder. "He's exhausted. He needs to rest."

She nods wordlessly. She carries Gabriel into his bedroom and lays him gently on the bed. He is asleep in minutes.

Isaac watches from the doorway. His eyes fall to the empty cradle. "What do you suppose Hales was doing on Leach's ship?"

Caroline laces her fingers through her son's. "It doesn't matter. He helped Gabriel get to safety. That's all that's important."

"Of course it matters! They must have been working together. Hales knew how to find Leach's ship. Knew how to find his house." He folds his arms behind his head, his thoughts charging. "But if he were working with Leach, why would he have come to see you last night? Why help Gabriel escape?"

For a long time, Caroline doesn't speak. "Perhaps he had a change of heart," she says finally. Her voice is cold, as though she is angry Isaac has dared to ask these questions. "Perhaps he doesn't have it in him to be that brutal man he was hoping to be."

When Scarlett climbs back up to the bar, everything is quiet. Isaac and Caroline have taken Gabriel home. Flora has disappeared upstairs. But Jamie; he is still here.

She stands with her back pressed against the front door. She does not know what to think. Does not know how to feel. Gabriel is safe. Mary is still missing. Jamie has looked into the smuggling tunnel.

His footsteps come towards her.

"I'm sorry," she says instinctively. Sorry for what? Sorry for who her father is? Sorry for helping her brother pay off their debts? Sorry for not fighting harder when Charles Reuben had first slipped a tobacco rasp into her hand and told her to run it up the hill beneath the riding officers' noses? She doesn't know. She just wishes she were a better person.

"I knew what I was bringing you home to," says Jamie. He is close, his voice making something warm in her chest. He takes a step and he is closer still, his breath tickling her nose.

Scarlett's fingers tense around her skirts. "You ought to…" She can't get the words out.

Leave. Before you see the knife in my skirts. Before you see more of the darkness in me than you already have.

How can he stay? How can he see?

She is not gripping her skirts anymore, she realises. She is gripping the sea-hardened edges of his coat.

He doesn't leave. Instead, he presses a kiss into her lips that makes her murmur with its suddenness. His stubble grazes her, hot and sharp. And her lips part beneath his, wanting more of him.

It is at once both gentle and forceful. And it makes her see the glaring imperfections of every other kiss she has ever had.

Too soon, he pulls away. Her pulse is fast and her skin is hot. And this thing has just become infinitely more difficult.

"Why did you do that?" she demands, her fists still tight around the hems of his jacket. "Why didn't you leave?"

His palm is pressed to her cheek, warm and rough and scented with sea. "I can't leave." She hears a smile in his voice. "You're blocking the door."

She tugs him closer, unsure what else to do. She just knows she wants him near.

The brass knocker beats against the door. Scarlett is grateful for the interruption. Grateful for something to take her attention from the terrifying race of her heart.

She clicks open the door.

"The dory," Isaac asks, marching inside. "Which way did it come from? Which way was Gabriel rowing?"

"I saw it coming around the point," says Jamie. "He must have come from the west."

"From Polruan." Isaac begins to pace.

Scarlett follows the sound. Left to right, left to right. "Can he tell you anything about where he was when he left the ship?" she asks.

"Nothing of any use."

"Leach must be close," says Scarlett. "Gabriel couldn't have rowed far on his own."

"Leach would have moved the moment he discovered Gabriel had escaped." Isaac keeps pacing. "Gone back towards Polruan, perhaps. He knows the river better than anyone."

"That may be," says Scarlett, "but you're far more intelligent. Wherever he is, you'll find him. I know you will." And when they do? How far will Leach go for retribution? The thought is too horrible to follow far.

She hears footsteps come down the stairs.

"Any word?" Flora asks. "Was Gabriel able to tell you

anything?"

"He says Asher Hales helped him escape. He and Leach must have been working together. I don't know how else Hales would have known how to find the ship."

Scarlett opens her mouth to speak. Isaac needs to know, surely, that Asher had paid a visit to their cottage that night. But what if she is wrong? What if she had misheard? Everything has been unsteady since her sight had been taken away. Her hearing is strangely heightened, and she is not certain she can trust it.

Isaac says: "Reuben wants me to meet a merchant on the river tonight."

Scarlett's shoulders stiffen. She is glad Isaac is confiding in her. But she cannot bear to imagine what thoughts are charging through Jamie's head.

"You ought to make the run. We need to keep Reuben on side." Her words are short and sharp. Conversation over. But Isaac says:

"You're right." He stops pacing. "I could use an extra pair of hands," he says to Jamie. "If you—"

"No." Scarlett's heart leaps into her throat. "No, Isaac, he can't."

"It's all right, Scarlett," says Jamie. "If—"

"No," she says, louder. She grips Jamie's arm. "You should go back to Polperro. Please."

He hesitates. "If you need me I'll be at the inn," he says after a moment.

Scarlett nods stiffly. She chews her lip, listening to his footsteps disappear.

"What was that about?" asks Isaac.

"He's not a sailor," Scarlett garbles. "He'll be of no use to you."

"He was of fine use when I went looking for Leach yesterday. Managed to find his feet."

"You can't take him!" she cries. "You can't." She drops her voice suddenly. "Promise me, Isaac."

"All right. All right. Calm yourself." He presses a hand to her shoulder, ushering her inside. "Let me see you upstairs."

Scarlett lets him walk her up the staircase. How she hates being chaperoned like this. She has become more of a burden to her family than she has ever been. But Isaac's nearness is steadying.

"You're going out searching?" she asks.

"Ayes." The parlour door squeaks as Isaac pushes it open. He ushers her inside. "Will's going to meet me at the harbour."

"Be safe," Scarlett murmurs. "Please." She wraps her arms around his neck and squeezes. The thought of her brother going charging after Tom Leach is terrifying. But she knows he has no choice.

She listens to him leave. Listens to the floorboards creak beneath his feet. Two sets of footsteps.

"Is Gabriel well?" Flora asks Isaac. They are in the hallway. At the top of the stairs perhaps. Flora's voice is hushed.

"He's exhausted and scared," he tells her. "But unharmed."

After a long pause, Flora says: "This is my doing. Leach has Mary because of me. I should never have turned him over to the authorities."

Scarlett cannot catch Isaac's response, but his voice is soft and gentle.

She creeps across the parlour, each footstep carefully placed so as not to make a sound. She presses an ear to the door.

"Please be careful," says Flora. "I couldn't bear to lose you."

Scarlett feels an intruder. This is not a conversation between friends. This is a conversation between two who care for each other deeply, desperately. Their half-whispered words are loving and secretive.

What is she not seeing, Scarlett wonders? Loving looks, gentle hands? Has their lifetime of friendship become something more?

Perhaps Caroline is not the only one hiding things.

PRECIOUS INFORMATION

Caroline hears footsteps. She climbs from Gabriel's bed and goes to the kitchen, pulling the nursery door closed behind her.

Isaac has returned from the inn. Caroline's heart thuds. She is terrified each time he speaks with his sister. There is so much Scarlett could tell him.

Gabriel had rowed from the west, he says. From the direction of Polruan. The direction of the river.

He tells her nothing else.

If Scarlett truly knows their father is alive, why has she not told her brother? Caroline has no thought of it, but she is slightly buoyed by the silence. Whatever her reasons, it seems Scarlett wants to keep this vital piece of knowledge to herself.

Isaac takes his scarf from the back of a chair and bundles it around his neck. "Will's agreed to meet me at the harbour," he tells Caroline. "I'll set sail the moment he arrives."

She nods. Takes the poker and jabs at the fire. Sparks fly up the chimney.

Isaac needs to know about Avery's money. If he finds Tom Leach's ship tonight, that information might be his only leverage to keep the man from harming their daughter.

Asher Hales had promised to tell Leach of the haul. But Asher Hales cannot be trusted.

That precious information may be all that is keeping Mary alive. It cannot be left in the hands of a liar.

Isaac picks up the woollen gloves he had left on the hearth to dry. He stuffs them into the pocket of his coat.

Caroline draws in her breath. She must tell him.

Now.

That precious piece of information that could keep their daughter alive.

That precious piece of information that will see their marriage in pieces.

It must be done.

She looks up at him. Feels suddenly dizzy. She grips the edge of the table. Isaac presses a steadying hand to her arm.

How can she do it? How can she face the interrogation that will surely follow? How can she bear to see that look of hate in her husband's eyes when he learns Jacob had been the one to tell her of the money?

It must be done.

"If you find Leach…" she begins. The words catch in her throat.

"I will find Leach," Isaac says firmly. "I'll not come back until I do." He grips her cheeks in his hands. "I'm going to bring Mary home. I swear it." He holds his lips against her forehead for a moment. Then he turns and marches from the house.

Caroline stumbles to the doorway. *Call after him*, she thinks. He needs to know. But by the time she finds her voice, he has already disappeared up the hill.

She goes back to Gabriel's bedside. Sits with her fingers laced through his. He is still sleeping deeply.

Her heart is fast. What kind of mother is she? How could she have been so selfish and cowardly when her own child's life is in danger? She closes her eyes as a tide of self-hatred sweeps over her.

She leaps to her feet at a knock at the door. Lets Asher inside hurriedly.

"Where is Mary?" she demands.

He is dressed the same ill-fitting clothes he had been the last time she had seen him. The long sleeves of his coat are folded ridiculously over his hands, his shirt stretched tight across his shoulders. His hair is tied back neatly.

He peers into the bedroom at Gabriel. "I'm glad he made it back safely."

"Where is Mary?" Caroline says again, her voice rising.

Asher raises his eyebrows. "This is all the thanks I get for helping your son escape?"

"Thanks? You were the one who took him in the first place!"

"No. That was Tom Leach."

At the mention of Leach's name, Caroline's throat tightens. She pulls closed the nursery door and lowers her voice. "Did you tell him of the money?"

Asher nods.

A strange sort of relief floods her.

"He's given you two days. You'll meet him at The Ship. You give him the money and he will give you your daughter."

141

Caroline presses a hand over her mouth to stop a sob escaping. Two days. The money will be near impossible to get to in such a short amount of time. But she must find a way. She sinks into a chair at the table, her legs suddenly unsteady.

"Where is it?" Asher asks.

Caroline stares at the floor. She does not want him to know. Does not want Asher Hales to be the man with whom she is sharing this secret. But she cannot do this alone. And there is no one else she can ask. "It's in the Mariner's Arms. In the wall of the cellar."

Asher's lips part. "The wall of the cellar?"

She nods. "There are bricks out of place close to the opening of the smuggling tunnel. You can see where the wall has been broken into."

"Why is it there?" The excitement in Asher's voice is thinly veiled.

"Jacob said Davey paid Flora's father to hide it in the inn. He was too scared to keep it in his own house. I suppose he was afraid of men coming after him." She stands, and begins to pace. "Tell Leach what I just told you. The haul's whereabouts in exchange for my daughter."

"Leach wants the money. Not just information."

"This is priceless information," Caroline hisses. "How can I get to that money?"

"You can get to it," says Asher. "You just can't get to it without telling people what you know."

Caroline's thoughts are racing. He is right. She can get to it. She must. There can be no other way.

She stands close to Asher. Looks into his eyes. She knows he still loves her. And she must use that. "I need your help," she says. "I need a boat. I need you to take me to the eastern beach tonight. Around to the mouth of the tunnel."

THE HEALING WELL

Scarlett appears at the door of the kitchen. The place is a chaos of potent scents; apples and nutmeg, ginger and cinnamon. "Lambswool?" she asks Flora.

"I hope so." Flora tosses the fruit into a pot of simmering ale. "The last batch was something of a disaster." She is jittery after the morning's events. Had needed something to keep herself occupied. When she had returned home after taking Bessie to school, she had gone straight to the kitchen and set the pot to boil.

"I'm glad of it," says Scarlett. "I was worried you were thinking to not reopen the inn."

Flora doesn't answer. The thought had crossed her mind. The Mariner's Arms has given her anxious nights, has led her to the lock-up. Letting the place fall into disrepair had felt fleetingly appealing. But she has worked far too hard to let the inn slide through her fingers.

She stirs the pot, then glances over her shoulder at Scarlett. "Are you all right?" she asks. "Is there something you need?"

"The well at Saint Cleer," says Scarlett. "Will you take me?"

They take a carriage from Polperro. The morning is misty and damp, the sun a perfect circle glowing behind the clouds.

They share the coach with three others; an elderly couple Flora has seen selling eggs at the market and a man in a tarred fishing coat who cracks his jaw with disturbing regularity.

Scarlett sits with her eyes turned to the window. A force of habit? Or is she trying to picture the world that is passing her by? Is she seeing the neatly trimmed hedges and the vast sweep of the moor? Does she see the engine houses of the tin mines blotting the purple-grey landscape?

At Liskeard they leave the coach and pay a farmer to take them to Saint Cleer.

Flora has given little credence to the stories of holy wells. They would be a fine thing to believe in, of course, these sacred springs that dot the country and bring back lost health and fortune. But she has always needed more than fervently spoken words in order to believe. She knows proof is something the desperate mind rarely bothers to seek.

But she has seen images in dark glass, has watched stones and rhymes heal her daughter. Perhaps there is magic in the water of the well.

Either way, it is not up to her to make such decisions on Scarlett's behalf.

Flora knows she is the one who ought to have suggested they make this journey. She has come to realise her mother's craft is something she needs in her life. Has come to realise the village healer is something she needs to be. But the things she had found in her mother's room have rattled her to the core.

She has doubts. Scepticism. And now she has begun to question the very decency of this thing she is beginning to build her life around.

She has trained herself to speak with conviction. But the people of Talland need a healer who truly believes. A healer who can swear by her cures, without fearing she is crossing some boundary into darkness. Without belief, without faith, what is she but a charlatan?

Believing in the magic of healing wells opens up far too many possibilities. If there is magic in the world, it means there is far more power in her mother's chest than Flora had first believed. It means she has the ability to see tomorrow, and all the responsibilities that come with that. It means there is the possibility that hastily scrawled circle on the guestroom floor has the power to conjure up something unwanted. And it means there is the chance her husband does not lie quiet in his grave.

Flora knows that if she is to be a successful healer, she needs to embrace this world, understand it; the light and the dark. She is not sure she has the courage. Nor is she sure she has the skills. She has not helped Scarlett, has not helped Caroline. The only place the craft has led her of late has been to discover things about her mother she does not want to know.

She shifts uncomfortably as the farmer's wagon lurches over a rut in the road.

Scarlett says: "How long have you been sharing my brother's bed?"

Flora feels suddenly, foolishly hot. "It's finished," she says. "That's all that matters." The words leave a hollowness inside her. She picks at a scrap of beeswax beneath her fingernail.

"You love him." Scarlett's tone is matter-of-fact, not accusatory.

Flora looks out the window. The spire of Saint Cleer's church is cutting into the cloud bank. "What does that matter?" she says finally.

Scarlett reaches out and loops her hand through Flora's arm.

They sit in silence until the wagon clatters to a halt.

Hemmed by vast moorland and ancient stones, the village of Saint Cleer seems to straddle this world and another. Wind ripples the grass, vivid green between stone cottages and curving mud-black roads. Clouds hang low, threatening to open.

The farmer points down the street. "The well's on the corner. Past the village green." He glances at Scarlett. "You need help getting there?"

"I can manage," she says brusquely. She clenches her jaw with determination.

Flora's stomach tightens. Scarlett has too much faith. There is a belief in her, Flora knows, that when they make the journey home, she will be seeing those engine houses for real. How far will she fall if the water fails her?

The well sits among the grass on the edge of the narrow street, presided over by unkempt trees and a worn Celtic cross. With Scarlett gripping her arm, Flora steps carefully over the low stone fence, aware she is navigating for both of them.

The path to the water is well worn. The sick and desperate have been coming here for centuries, Flora knows. People have knelt on this bank seeking cures for black death, cures for the sweating sickness. Madmen have been dipped beneath the water in hope it might restore their sanity.

Flora has been here once before, as a young girl, when her mother had accompanied one of the villagers to the well to seek relief from consumption. Had the water worked that day? Flora had never thought to question it.

The air is still, cold. All she can hear is the murmuring echo of water against stone.

Scarlett draws in her breath. "Take me to the edge."

Scarlett kneels on the wet grass and reaches down into the water. She hears it bubbling, moving beneath her.

She needs to believe. She has become afraid of the dark. Has become afraid she'll not survive it.

She reaches into the well and cups a handful of water, bringing it to her face. She lets the drops run down her cheeks. She holds her breath, waiting for the light, the clouds, the crooked spire of the church.

She sees nothing. Below her, the water keeps moving. Keeps bubbling.

Is this a sign the well has failed? Do the sick who touch this water emerge instantly healed? Do madmen step from the bowsenning pool with their senses intact?

Why has it forsaken her? Is she not a good enough person? Has a lifetime of smuggling and light fingers rendered her immune to the healing water? Has she gone too far into the dark to ever be pulled back?

She reaches for her bonnet. Her throat tightens, but she will not cry.

To cry is to admit defeat.

In the carriage, she says aloud: "The water will work. I know it will. Perhaps it will just take time." She hears the waver in her voice. Forces it away.

"Yes," says Flora. "Perhaps."

The cart wheels hiss as they carve through the mud. Scarlett grips the edge of the bench to keep her balance. That pain in her throat is there again, her tears close to spilling. She swallows and swallows, forcing the pain and the tears away.

Flora says: "You have a man who cares for you very much."

Scarlett knows she is only speaking of such things to distract her. But the mention of Jamie makes something flare inside her. The feeling is half pleasant, half terrifying. And entirely unfamiliar.

Involuntarily, she brings a hand to her mouth, feeling the place his lips had touched hers. A kiss after seeing the Wild, after seeing the smuggling tunnel.

What had he been thinking? Why had he not ridden away?

She had learned so much of him on their journey from Portreath. A childhood of farming and folk tales and summers in the sea. She knows he hates spiders, knows he drinks mahogany. Knows he'd happily eat taddago pies for every meal. And yet she knows not a thing of his work, beyond the glimpses she had seen in Portreath. What had driven him to fight smuggling? Has he faced men willing to kill to keep their hauls hidden? How many free traders has he seen imprisoned, transported, impressed?

Each time their conversation had veered in that direction, they had pulled it back to safer ground. Scarlett is acutely aware they are keeping things from each other. Hiding away the parts of their lives that make them incompatible.

She winds her shawl around her finger. The edge is damp with well water.

"You're worried," says Flora, "of having a future with him if your sight does not return."

"Is that what you think? That my sight will not return?" She tries to keep her voice steady.

"I don't know, Scarlett. I'm sorry."

Flora's bluntness is a fist to the stomach, but Scarlett is grateful for her honesty. She tugs her shawl tight around her shoulders.

"Jamie is a riding officer," she blurts.

And this, she realises, is the way to shoot a conversation dead. She understands the silence, of course. Jamie had walked through Flora's inn. He had climbed into the cellar and seen the tunnel.

Jamie could have them all before the magistrate.

"I see," says Flora, after far too long. "And can we…"

"We can trust him," Scarlett says shortly. She entangles her hands tighter in her shawl. Flora's silence tells her what she has known in the back of her mind all along; that she and Jamie are anything but well-matched. "I shouldn't have said anything," she mumbles. "But I just needed to tell someone."

"He seems a good man," says Flora, finding her voice. "Truly. You ought to keep him close."

Scarlett allows herself a faint smile. Flora's words are reassuring. Because ill-matched or not, she desperately does not want Jamie to ride away. Just how insurmountable, she finds herself wondering, can their differences be?

"Will you take me to the Three Pilchards?" she asks. "I need to see him."

CONFESSION

Jamie sits in the corner of the tavern, his officer's journal on the table in front of him. He records the details of the shooting in the castle ruins, and of Tom Leach's fleeting image through the hole in the keep. Records the search for the man he had undertaken in Isaac Bailey's lugger.

He looks up to find Scarlett standing over him. She is wearing her cloak and woollen bonnet, her pale blue skirts streaked with mud. She smells of earth and water.

"Jamie?" she says. "Are you there?"

He touches her hand. "How did you find me?"

"Flora brought me here." She sits beside him, her fingers grazing the notebook. "Is that your journal?"

He closes the book. "Yes."

"Am I in there?" she asks. "Did you write of the thieving woman from Talland you trapped on the beach?"

Jamie smiles. "No. I assumed you didn't want such a thing on record."

"Take me up to your room," she says suddenly.

He swallows. "I can't, Scarlett." He keeps his voice low.

"People will talk. They'll think badly of you."

More to the point, if he has her in his room, his control will likely slip through his fingers. And that would make this far more complicated than it already is.

"The people in this place know the kind of person I am." Scarlett winds her shawl around her hands. "Please. I just need to speak with you. About things it would be dangerous for stray ears to overhear."

Jamie does not want to speak. Speaking is far too difficult. There can be no more avoiding the issues they have been dancing around.

A big part of him longs for her. Wants nothing more than to whisk her up to his room and feel her move beneath him. Wants nothing more than to wake every morning beside her. But can they truly have a life together when it feels necessary to hide so much from each other?

Smuggling is not a choice, she had told him. A thing she had been forced into by her father. And yet when he had caught her on the beach in Portreath, she'd not been acting on her father's bidding. She had been acting for no one but herself. Had turned to smuggling as a means of making money. She had grabbed at a dishonest solution, instead of trying to earn herself an honest wage.

There was a part of him that had wanted to string her up for it. Wanted to show her there was no place for smugglers on his scrap of Cornwall's coast. And by right, he ought to have done it. There are few riding officers foolish enough to turn down the chance at a conviction. But there are also few riding officers foolish enough to lose their head over a woman with smuggled tobacco in her cloak.

He cannot stay here at the inn forever. One day soon he will be forced to make a decision. Commit or ride away.

He takes her upstairs. Unlocks the door and guides her inside. The room is small and cramped, with a narrow bed against one wall and a table and single chair in the corner. He leads Scarlett to the bed, then sits opposite her on the chair. Her knees are an inch from his. He can feel the heat rising from her body.

She takes off her bonnet and sits it on the bed beside her. Beneath it, her hair is a windswept snarl. She folds her hands in her lap. Inhales. "My brother conducts free trading runs for the syndicate boss to pay off our father's debts," she says. "He added a false bottom to his lugger so he can slide smuggled goods beneath the revenue men's noses. He uses the tunnel beneath the Mariner's Arms to bring them in from the beach." Her voice drops a little. "We are all involved. I run the goods to buyers, and carry the signalling lantern. Flora stores the contraband in her cellar. Caroline has adulterated smuggled tea and sold it to unsuspecting buyers. And half the village is in Isaac's landing party."

Jamie doesn't speak at once. This should infuriate him, of course. He has spent countless nights intercepting deliveries, has lost friends to smugglers' bullets. But he is grateful for her honesty, her openness.

He reaches for her hand. He closes his eyes, wanting to experience this as she is. The warmth of their skin pressing against each other's, the steady thud of his heart.

He opens his eyes. Her hand looks small and fragile in his. He knows it an illusion. There is little fragility to this woman.

He tells her. Tells her of his training, the careful planning of his patrols, the oath he had sworn at Customs House. He tells her of the letters passed along the coast between officers, and of the way the army so often refuses to assist with their raids. He tells her of his desire to see the country cleansed of the dishonest blight that has seized it.

"Why?" she asks. "Why such hatred for free trade? Did smugglers steal from you? Kill your family? What?"

"No." He shifts uncomfortably. She has been honest with him, and he will do the same for her. "I despise it because it's wrong, Scarlett. That's all. It's dishonest and wrong."

"Yes," she says after a moment. "I know it is." She tries to slide her hand from his, but he doesn't release his grip.

"Why are you still here?" she asks. "You've been away from Portreath for more than four days. Your commanding officer will not be happy."

"No. But how can I leave without knowing your brother's children are safe? How can I just ride away?"

"That's why you're here? Because you want to help my brother find his children?"

Jamie says: "It's far more than that."

And suddenly she is standing over him, her knees threaded between his, strands of her hair tickling his cheek. Her hands are sliding over his shoulders, his chest, feeling the shape of him. Her lips finds his. She is forceful, possessive. Seems to care little where such a thing might lead.

This is far too dangerous.

"Scarlett," he manages, desire thickening his voice, "we can't. I'll not take you before you're married."

His words drop heavily into the silence.

How has this conversation brought them here?

Scarlett is young, strong-willed and clever. Despite all that has befallen her, Jamie is sure she soon will marry. Soon there will be a man waking each morning beside her. And he will have to decide if he is brave enough, strong enough for that man to be him.

She slides out of his arms and sits back on the edge of the

bed. Knots her fingers together. "And if Isaac finds Mary? If he brings her home safely? What will you do then? Will you go back to Portreath?"

For several moments, he says nothing. He does not want to leave. But a part of him is afraid to stay. How can he hold a position in the revenue service and have a future with this woman?

"Do you wish you'd stayed in Portreath?" she asks.

"No." He does not need to think.

And then he sees. If he does not take his chance to be the man who wakes up beside her, it will be someone else. And Jamie realises how desperately he does not want that to be the case.

He takes her face in his hands, directs her gaze.

Here. Look at me.

"If Isaac finds Mary, then yes, I will leave," he tells her. "I love my job. I want to return to it."

No, not *want*. *Need* to return to it.

He is aware of what he is really saying. *I need to fight this life you have built. I need to punish those who do what you do.*

He is aware of what he is really saying, and he is aware of the absurdity of it. Because what he says next is: "But I would like nothing more than for you to come back to Portreath with me."

I would like you to come back to Portreath with me and watch as I do these things. I would like you to come back to Portreath and listen as I relay stories of midnight patrols and hard-fought court cases. I want to sit at the supper table beside you and tell you every moment of every day.

Absurdity of course. But how desperately he wants a life in which he returns to his cottage each night to find her in it.

Scarlett makes a noise in her throat. Is this happiness?

Disappointment? He can't read her. She stands suddenly and wraps her arms around his neck, pushing her body hard against his. "The healing well failed," she says. "My sight might never return." Her voice is muffled by his hair.

"I don't care." He'd had no thought of it. Her blindness is the smallest of the divides they will have to cross.

He is asking a lot of her, he knows. Asking her to leave her family, her home. Asking her to leave behind the world she knows. And for what? To be a riding officer in trade-drenched Cornwall is no easy thing. There is constant distrust, constant whispers behind his back. There is the curse of looking at everyone and wondering what they are hiding. There are the conversations that stop when he and his colleagues walk into taverns. There are friends who tell him only half truths.

A life by his side will not be easy.

If Scarlett is to turn him down, he will not blame her. But he needs her to know how he feels.

No need for an answer now, he tells her, pushing her tangled hair behind her ears. The future is so hazy, so uncertain, that to answer now would be impossible. But he is glad there is to be no more hiding.

He kisses her gently. "I'll take you back to the inn."

"Not yet," says Scarlett. "Just let me stay a while."

He lays back on the bed and pulls her down with him. Her hand slides over his chest, coming to rest above the place his heart is drumming. She rests her head against his shoulder. And he closes his eyes against the last threads of daylight that are filtering into the room.

GHOSTS IN SHADOWS

"What's wrong, Mammik?" Bessie asks, as she and Flora walk back over the cliffs from the charity school. Smears of pink sky push through the thick bank of cloud. Wind whips their hair against their cheeks.

Flora slides an arm around her daughter's shoulder. "I'm sorry, *cheel-vean*." She has been distracted since returning from Saint Cleer that afternoon. In truth, she has been distracted since Scarlett had kicked open the guestroom. Has found herself raking through memories of her mother, analysing, overthinking.

She takes Bessie's hand and keeps walking past the inn.

"Where are we going?"

"We're going visiting." Flora knocks on Martha Francis's door.

Martha opens the door a crack, her face breaking into a

156

smile at the sight of them. She ushers them inside, pressing wrinkled hands to Bessie's cheeks and planting a wet kiss on her forehead.

"Mammik said we're going visiting," Bessie announces.

"Visiting? I see." Martha looks past her at Flora. "Is everything all right?"

Flora manages a faint smile. She feels suddenly foolish. Has she really let the carving on the floor rattle her so much?

But she needs to know what her mother had been doing in that guestroom. And she needs to know why. Perhaps Martha will not have the answers. But Flora can think of no one else to ask.

Martha plants Bessie by the hearth with a cup of milk and an enormous slice of saffron cake. She hangs the kettle over the fire and nods for Flora to sit.

Flora perches on the edge of a chair at the kitchen table. Edgily, she picks at the wax on the rim of the candleholder. "You knew my mother well, ayes?"

Martha smiles. "Yes, of course. Meg and I were dear friends."

"You came to her for help a lot, didn't you. For charms and the like."

Another nod.

Flora watches Bessie break the end off her cake and cram it into her mouth. "You trusted her then? You trusted the charms she gave you?" The words feel bitter on her tongue. Feel like a betrayal. Is she truly asking such things about her mother? The woman she remembers as being nothing but caring and selfless?

Martha doesn't speak at once. "What's brought this on, Flora?" she asks gently.

Flora sighs. "I opened up one of the guestrooms in the inn.

And I found some things inside. Things my mother warned me away from when I was a child." She sucks in her breath. "Things the vicar would class as black magic."

"Ah." Martha looks unsurprised.

"You know something of it."

Martha spoons tea into the pot. "You know what your mother was like, *cheel-vean*. You know easily she got carried away. You've a much more level head on your shoulders than she ever did."

Flora manages a pale smile. She is not sure this is true.

"Meg saw something in her black mirror one day," says Martha, the teaspoon dangling from her fingers. "Something that terrified her."

"Something in the mirror?" Flora repeats. "What was it?"

"She wouldn't say. But whatever it was, she were desperate not to see it come true. Told me she were doing her best to reverse what she had seen. Said she knew an enchantment that could stop it happening."

"Counter-sorcery."

"Ayes, I suppose that's what it were."

Flora sighs. "I thought her wiser than that."

"Don't think ill of her," Martha says gently. "It was a difficult time for her. She'd just lost your father. She wasn't thinking clearly. She made a mistake, is all. And she knew it too."

"What do you mean?"

Martha's voice becomes low and conspiratorial. "Poor woman scared herself silly. She were convinced she were seeing things. Ghosts and demons hiding in that room where she made the enchantment."

Flora leans back in her chair. She thinks of her mother walking through the inn, her husband dead, her daughter asleep; in that dark, lonely place Flora herself has been far too many times. How easy it is, she knows, to let imagination get the better of you in such a place.

She pictures her mother staring into the mirror, her eyes distant, her pale hair falling over her shoulders. Her mother had believed staunchly in the power of the dark glass. Had trusted that tomorrow would appear beneath its surface. What had she seen to rattle her so much? What had been so dreadful she had sought to reverse it by venturing into dark enchantments and counter-sorcery?

In her mind's eye, Flora sees her mother driving a knife across the wall of the guestroom. She imagines her face contorted in fear, as her grieving, terrified mind found demons in the empty shadows of the inn. Imagines her locking the door of the tainted room and throwing away the key.

Flora rubs her eyes. The creaking passages of the inn, she knows well, have the power to take away rationality. How she wishes she could hold her mother, just for a moment, and tell her not to let her feverish mind carry her away.

"The black magic," she says. "She did it only to try and change what she saw? There was no other reason? There was nothing spiteful about it?" She looks into her hands. "She was not seeking to punish anyone? Lay a curse?"

Martha takes the kettle from the hook above the fire and pours boiling water into the teapot. "Of course not," she says gently. "You know who your mother was, Flora. You know she only ever used the craft to help people. Never to harm them."

Yes. Of course. Flora feels a stab of guilt that she has dared think otherwise. Her mother had been the most devoted of healers. Had always done all she could to help the people of Talland. Perhaps her work had angered the vicar, but Flora has come to realise that such a thing is easily done.

That evening, she goes to the churchyard with a bunch of heather in her hand. She takes the withered stems from her mother's grave and lays fresh flowers in their place.

HIDING PLACES

Isaac grips the wheel of the lugger. The wind is cold against his cheeks, but he is blazing inside. They are slicing through the sea towards the mouth of the river. The silhouette of the merchant ship peeks out of the gloom.

They had spent the morning combing the coast, tracing the outlines of beaches that appear and vanish with the tide. When there had been no sign of Leach's ship, they had made their way onto the river, squeezing the lugger down tree-lined narrows and tight, muddy offshoots.

And now, Reuben's rendezvous. Ten cases of cognac and Burgundy wine to be stored beneath the bulkheads.

Isaac is furious at the interruption. But he cannot risk Reuben's anger. Cannot risk making any more enemies.

Will stands beside him on the foredeck, turning up the collar of his coat against the wind. The sun has slipped into the water, leaving only cloud-drenched moonlight. "I've told the landing party to be ready on the eastern beach," he says. "They'll take the goods into the tunnel."

"Forget the landing party. I'm not going back until I have Mary."

"I know," says Will. "I know. But what if we find her after we've made this exchange? We can't bring the lugger back to port full of contraband. We'll be stuck at sea until we can get word to the landing party. Best they're ready and waiting."

Will is right, of course. The revenue men are watching Talland far too closely for them to be haphazard with their landings. The last time Customs had inspected the ship, they had been dangerously close to uncovering the false bottom in the hold.

"I'll go aboard," says Will, as they draw closer to the merchant.

"You don't have to—"

"You're a mess, Isaac. Better way I make the transaction. You stay here and help me get the goods aboard." He is lowering the dory before Isaac can argue. Climbs down the ladder and steps into the boat.

Isaac stands at the wheel, feeling the lugger shift on the waves. He looks over his shoulder towards the blue mouth of the river. The water is dark and silky, curling away towards the hills.

His stomach turns over. Leach will have discovered Gabriel's escape by now, surely. Will he have taken his anger out on Mary? At the thought, he feels suddenly, violently ill. He closes his eyes and tries to breathe.

His knuckles whiten around the wheel. The moment the lugger is loaded, he will head back onto the river; a warren of murky tributaries and dark snarls. That black ship must be hiding in there somewhere. And he is not leaving this place until he finds it.

In the darkness, Caroline can make out the inky shape of Asher on the landing beach. He paces, arms wrapped around himself to keep out the cold. A dory sits at the edge of the water, waves slapping against its hull.

Caroline looks back over her shoulder at the village. She has left Martha Francis watching over Gabriel. Had hated to leave him. But what choice does she have?

"The boat," she says. "How did you get it? Did you steal it from the harbour?"

"No. I purchased it." Asher snorts. "Of course I stole it."

Caroline holds out the pick she had found among Isaac's gardening tools. "Will this work?"

Asher takes the pick. "It ought to break down the wall, yes. But I don't know how you expect to do this without anyone hearing you. You'd best hope the inn is empty."

Caroline swallows heavily. Before she had come to the beach, she had ventured down the hill to the Mariner's Arms. A lamp had been flickering in one of the windows. Flora and Bessie will be there for certain. And Scarlett?

Caroline steps into the boat. If she is to be discovered, so be it. "Just take me around the point."

Asher shoves hard against the dory and it slides through the sand, gliding onto the surface of the sea. He climbs over the gunwale and sits opposite Caroline. She turns her head to avoid meeting his eyes.

She will find the money tonight. She has no choice but to do so.

But as she had spent the day piecing together her plans to unearth the silver, she had also pieced together her plans to let Asher Hales carry the blame.

It was Asher who had discovered the hiding place, she will tell Isaac, when he demands to know how she came to know of these riches. Had discovered its whereabouts on his journey to Portreath. Gleaned the information from an unnamed man. And she had threatened him, she will say. Threatened a cowardly man into giving up his knowledge.

She sickens herself with these lies. But lies are far less painful than the truth. The thought of Isaac looking into her eyes and seeing who she really is sickens her to the core.

A cold breeze skims across the water, splintering the reflection of the moon. Caroline pulls her cloak tighter around her. Her breath is silver as it rises into the night.

Asher pulls on the oars. The dory slides soundlessly around the point. And there is the eastern beach. Though she has been in Talland for more than a decade, it is the first time Caroline has seen it.

Asher rows towards the shore, leaping into the water and shoving the boat up the sand. He offers his hand to help her climb from the boat. Ignoring him, she clutches her skirts in her fist and steps into the shallow water, exhaling sharply at the coldness of the sea.

She trudges up the beach, squinting to make out the contours of the rock face ahead of them. The mouth of the tunnel is invisible in the dark. She trails a hand across the cliff, stopping when she feels it fall away beneath her fingers.

"Here." She crouches low, her skirts in her fist. As she steps into the rock, the pale moonlight vanishes, leaving her in impenetrable blackness. It is a sudden, disorienting sensation. She presses a hand against the wall to guide her.

Asher is close behind; his footsteps crunching, his breath fast. Caroline feels the earth gather in her throat.

And then there is no more rock, just the smooth wooden plane of the barrels blocking the tunnel entrance. She throws her body weight against them, making them groan along the floor.

She steps into the cellar or the Mariner's Arms.

"There's a lantern by the stairs," Asher tells her under his breath.

Little point him being so silent, Caroline thinks wryly, feeling her way through the darkness. The moment they slam the pick into the wall of the cellar, they will be heard. Flora will come, perhaps Scarlett. She must have her story ready.

Asher will deny it all, of course. He will argue, and he will hurl accusations. Caroline can only hope there is enough lingering trust in Flora and Scarlett for them to believe her over him.

She finds the lamp, lighting it with a trembling hand. She carries it across the cellar, holding it up to the wall beside the tunnel. The flame is hot against her cheek.

"Here," she tells Asher. "The bricks have been replaced. It looks as though there's something behind them."

He nods silently, his eyes wide. He has been searching for this wealth almost half his life. And here he stands before its hiding place.

He will not get his hand on a single coin.

Every scrap of this haul must go to Leach to spare her baby's life.

What will Asher Hales do if they discover the money tonight? Caroline knows he is selfish, fixated on his dreams. Knows there is every chance he will take the silver and run. Does he love her enough to put Mary's life ahead of his own?

She doubts it.

But she needs him. Needs him to strike the rock, just as she had needed him to row the boat around the point. To this whole sorry operation, Asher Hales is frustratingly necessary.

Caroline holds up the lamp and nods towards the wall. "Do it."

Flora rifles through the chaos of the kitchen cupboard until she finds a ream of shagreen at the bottom. She runs a finger over the coarse animal hide. It will do well for smoothing away the carvings in the guestroom.

She rubs the shagreen over the wall, beginning to smooth down the letters. A part of her regrets planing away this scrap of her mother. But these letters must be erased. Like it or not, she must open this place to guests soon, just as she must do with her mother's room, Jack's room.

When Isaac has found Mary, she tells herself. When Scarlett is healed. Then she will open the tavern doors again. Then she will open these rooms. She will hire workers. Men and women to run the bar. And she will dedicate herself to caring for her guests. The Mariner's Arms will be a place she can be proud of. A place Jack would have been proud of. She feels a swell of determination.

The black mirror is leaning up against the wall where Scarlett had left it.

And in the corner of her eye, Flora sees it.

Firelight in the glass.

She has seen this many times; flames dancing over the black surface of the mirror. But now a chill runs through her.

Because this is no reflection. The fireplace in this room has sat cold and disused for more than twenty years.

She lifts the mirror, unable to pull her eyes from it. She looks closer. And she realises exactly what she is seeing.

She tosses the mirror in shock. It shatters on the floor, black glass spraying across the room, lodging in the indents of her mother's magic circle. Flora steps backwards, stumbling hard into the wall.

And she stops. Feels the floorboards bend beneath her feet. She looks down. Here in this corner, the boards are a darker colour than the rest of the room. There are large gaps between them and she can feel a cold draught gusting through. She goes to the parlour for the fire poker. Shoves the tip of it in the gap between the boards and wrenches hard. One snaps loudly, revealing a dark recess beneath the floor.

She stops. Is there noise below her as well?

She waits. Yes, a crashing, a splintering in the cellar, two storeys beneath her feet. At the end of the passage, Bessie's dog barks.

Flora draws in her breath. Is she to let herself fall for this again? This trickery of the tunnel? Crashing, splintering; yes, she had heard that the day Jack had died. These sounds are nothing more than her memory playing tricks. She tries to push the noise away.

She shoves the poker between the floorboards again. Another falls away. She shines the lamp into the space beneath the floor. Mice scurry into dark corners, escaping the sudden beam of light. Bessie's dog races into the room, yapping, circling, trying to push his way past her.

In the space beneath the floorboards is a cloth bag. Flora shines the light over it, wary of its contents. In her time, her mother had packaged all manner of things into bags;

hangman's rope and earth from a grave, fingernails and blackened animal hearts. She cannot tell what is inside.

She reaches down and lifts it carefully. It is small, no bigger than an apple. Heavy. She opens the bag and inhales sharply. Silver. It glitters faintly in the lamplight.

A mythical treasure. A thing Flora had not believed in. So much of her world, she is coming to realise, is made up of things she does not believe in.

She sets the floorboards back over the hole and takes the bag into the parlour. She sits on the edge of the armchair to inspect the coins more closely. They are rough-hewn silver, foreign characters imprinting surfaces worn smooth. The bag is heavy in her lap.

And there is more thumping, more splintering. If these sounds are otherworldly, this other world is coming far too close. Flora know Isaac's landing party will soon be arriving on the beach, ready to bring the latest haul through the tunnel. But this is not the sound of the landing party.

Clutching the bag of silver, she makes her way down into the cellar. Lamplight flickers at the bottom of the stairs.

And there is Caroline, sitting amongst the broken furniture. A dust-covered pick lies on the floor. Beside the mouth of the tunnel, the brick wall of the cellar has been hacked at, revealing an empty cavity carved into the rock.

Flora stares.

She had been certain she knew every inch of the inn. Knew every passage, every brick, every corner, every shadow. But how foreign this place seems now, with its carvings and cavities and its treasures beneath the floor. She feels oddly betrayed.

Caroline doesn't look at her. "It was supposed to be here. I was to give it to Leach. In exchange for Mary's life." She stands shakily. "But it's a myth. It's all a lie."

The steps creak beneath Flora's feet. "It's not a myth." She holds out the pouch.

Caroline stares at it for a moment. She takes it and peeks inside, her lips parting with shock. "It was supposed to be in the cellar wall. That's where your father put it."

"How do you know that?"

Caroline doesn't answer.

"You came looking for it. How did you know it was in my inn? Who told you?"

Caroline tries to step past. Tries to reach the door.

No, she is not leaving. Not like this. Not without answers.

Flora's hand shoots out and grabs her wrist. There is no trust between them, of course. How can there be? There is no trust, but there is this shimmering silver secret.

"Who else knows of this?" Flora asks sharply. "Who else can I expect to find treasure hunting in my cellar?"

"No one."

"How did you learn of this? Who told you it was here?" It is not just about her and Bessie's safety, Flora realises. She needs to know who these people are who understand the Mariner's Arms better than she does. Needs to know how they had come to learn of this secret. This silver that had shown itself to her at the very moment Caroline had gone looking. The inn, it seems, had wanted to give up its secrets tonight.

Flora feels her hand tighten involuntarily around Caroline's wrist. "Tell me. I need to know."

Caroline pulls away sharply. "You don't need to know a thing." She stands close to Flora, her eyes flashing. "You'll tell no one. Do you understand?" She slips the pouch inside her cloak. "After all you've done to me, you will keep this to yourself."

A THING OF RETRIBUTON

The river narrows. There are trees and dark, trees and dark. A sliver of a moon shines off the water.

"Down here," says Isaac.

The lugger is sliding silently through the water, sails trimmed to catch the faint breath of wind.

Will shines the lantern down the thin corridor of water. "It's too narrow. We'll barely make it through. There's no way Leach would have managed to take the cutter this way."

"Down here," Isaac says again. "I'm sure of it."

He turns the wheel, feeling the hull grind against mud. He wills the lugger to keep moving, exhaling in relief as it rides the faint swell.

Down the tributary. Trees and dark.

And ahead of them is Leach's cutter. With its masts and hull painted black, it is little more than a shadow, anchored in the centre of the river.

What Isaac feels is not entirely relief. Not entirely

anticipation. Right now, he has hope that his daughter is alive. And he knows climbing aboard the ship could see that hope torn away forever.

He looks to Will. Wordlessly, they furl the sails, leaving the lugger to drift. Isaac uncoils the mooring ropes. He will secure the ship to one of the trees lining the river. Drop anchor here and the noise is bound to attract Leach's attention.

With the lugger secured, Isaac pockets his pistol and blows out the lamp. Light glows through the porthole of Leach's ship, picking out the gnarled trees at the edge of the river.

Isaac leaps from the ladder, landing in the shallow water close to the bank. He waits for Will to follow.

They trace the curve of the river, the water sighing around them with each laboured footstep. And they reach the black hull of the cutter. Isaac takes his pistol from his pocket, holding it above the waterline. He begins to wade towards the ladder. Water bubbles around his chest, the cold tightening his lungs. Will grabs his shoulder, holding him back.

"You can't just go charging onto the ship. You know Leach won't hesitate to shoot."

But what plan can be made? Without knowing the layout of the ship, they are just fumbling in the dark. Isaac's earlier reluctance has given way to urgency. He needs to get aboard the cutter as quickly as possible. There is no time for thought. No time to make plans.

He climbs the ladder and swings his legs over the gunwale, bringing streams of dark water with him. The deck is silent. The smell of pipe smoke hangs in the air, tinged with the murky breath of the river.

There is a hatch on the raised foredeck. Leading down to the saloon, Isaac guesses. It is tightly closed. He presses an ear to it. Through it he hears nothing.

171

A second hatch at the other end of the ship. It is open a crack and Isaac sees a faint light blinking beneath. He makes his way towards it and peeks through the gap. He sees a redheaded woman move beneath the hatch. He cannot tell if she is alone.

Tom Leach's wife. Jane. Isaac has seen the woman before. Seen her fawning over her husband at their cottage in Polruan.

He pulls on the hatch, cursing as it groans beneath his hands.

Jane looks up, swallowing a gasp of shock. Her eyes widen, but she doesn't speak. Doesn't scream. Does nothing to alert her husband.

Isaac lowers himself into the cabin. Jane watches silently, with her back pressed to the door.

Isaac's eyes dart around the room. He sees a tiny shape in the corner of the bunk, covered with a thin grey blanket. Motionless. He feels dizziness sweep over him. Is she sleeping? He is suddenly afraid to take a step. Afraid to go to her.

"Who are you?" Jane whispers.

Isaac steps towards the bunk. "I'm her father." He pulls back the blanket and sees the dark mop of Mary's hair. She lies on her front with her knees tucked beneath her, a fist curled beside her cheek. Isaac presses a soft hand to her back. He feels her body rise and fall with breath. The relief is so great he hears a sound come from his throat. He scoops her carefully from the bunk. It feels important not to wake her. To keep her blind to all that is happening. He closes his eyes for a moment, feeling the warmth of her as she burrows against his thudding chest.

When he looks back at Jane, there is a faint smile at the edge of her lips. "I did my best to care for her," she whispers.

"Keep her fed and warm."

Isaac gives a short nod. It doesn't feel right to thank her. "Where is your husband?" he asks under his breath.

"In the saloon. He has his weapon."

Isaac glances up at the hatch. He cannot climb back through with Mary in his arms. He will need to hand her back to Leach's wife. And he is not sure how far he can trust her.

Pistol in hand, he steps out into the saloon. Leach is sitting at the table, a pipe in one hand and a gun in the other. His pistol is trained on Will, who stands in the doorway, countering Leach's weapon with his own.

Isaac walks slowly towards him, eying the hatch leading back to the deck. On the edge of his vision, he sees Jane emerge from the cabin.

"Why?" he asks.

Leach sets his pipe in a bent tin ashtray. "It was a thing of retribution. But it's about so much more than that now."

"What are you talking about?"

Leach leans back against the bulkhead. "Your daughter for the silver your wife knows how to find."

"Don't involve my wife in this." Isaac feels Mary wriggle against his side. Feels her little hands clutch at his coat hem.

The corner of Leach's lips turn up. "You don't know," he says after a moment. "You don't know about that silver. But your father did."

"My father has been dead for years." Isaac's fingers tighten around his pistol. One bullet, he thinks, and the man would be dead. Retribution for his children, for his sister.

But how can he pull the trigger with Mary beneath his arm? She will not understand, of course, but she will see. She will hear. She will witness her father take another man's life. A part of her will carry it with her always.

Leach stands up from the table. "A haul of silver," he says. "Come to this place on a pirate ship. Hidden in your village. And your wife knows how to find it."

The claim makes Isaac feel strangely unsteady. But he shakes his head. A lie, of course. He and Caroline have lived in poverty their entire lives. If she had known such a thing, she would never have kept it from him.

His finger shifts on the trigger. No, he tells himself. Tom Leach is not worth the guilt that will follow. He does not want to leave a trail of blood behind him. He just wants to get his daughter home. Leach is outnumbered. Disadvantaged. Isaac steps towards the hatch.

Leach lurches suddenly and snatches his wife's arm. Yanks her in front of him and holds the pistol to her head. "Leave and I'll kill her."

"Go," Jane tells Isaac. "He'll not do it. I know he won't."

He can't risk it. Whatever faith this woman has in her husband's decency, Isaac does not share it. He glances at Will. They both have their guns firmly fixed on Leach. Beneath Isaac's arm, Mary shifts and whines.

In a sudden flash of movement, Will grabs the lantern hanging above the door and flings it across the cabin. The flame disappears, plunging the ship into darkness. Will rams a fist into the side of Leach's head. He stumbles forward into the table.

Isaac grabs Jane's wrist. "Come with us."

"No." She pulls free of his grip. "I can't."

"He'll kill you for letting me get to Mary."

"He won't. I trust him. I do."

Leach is climbing slowly to his feet. If his wife wants to face her husband's wrath, Isaac realises, he has no choice but to let her.

174

CLIFFTOPS

Scarlett can feel a strange restlessness to the place as Jamie walks her back over the hill to Talland. It is night now; she can tell by the emptiness of the streets, by the icy edge to the wind. She knows the landing party will be lining the cliffs and beaches, waiting, hoping for the return of Isaac's lugger.

Despite their earlier candidness, Scarlett wants Jamie back in Polperro before he catches sight of any of it. Him knowing how deeply she and her family are involved with smuggling is one thing. Him witnessing the whole event is quite another.

They reach the front door of the Mariner's Arms.

"You ought to get back," says Scarlett.

"Shall I see you upstairs?"

"I can manage." She feels in her pocket for the key Flora had given her.

Jamie holds her close, his lips to hers. Jamie who wants to take her back to Portreath. A thing she can't even begin to fathom right now.

She listens to his footsteps disappear. Stands in the doorway. The restlessness is within her, she realises. Disquiet brought about by her uselessness. She ought to be up on those cliffs with a signalling lantern, watching for Isaac's lugger.

How can she just sit at home and wait?

She calls up the stairs to Flora. She is going to the cottage. No, no I don't need help. Jamie is here.

She starts to walk. Feels the ground slope upwards. She finds the gate of the churchyard. She pushes hard and hears it creak beneath her hands.

She walks with her arm outstretched. Feels the smooth headstones graze her fingers. There is her mother, her brothers, her sisters. There is Jacob's memorial under which nothing but earth lies.

She stops walking. Listens. Is that the sigh of footsteps through the mud? Is the landing party here?

"Is someone there?" she calls, her voice low.

"Miss Bailey?"

She reaches a hand towards the voice. Makes contact with a man's thick chest.

"Who's there?"

"It's me. Ned Arthur."

Yes, Scarlett knows the man. A farmer from Isaac's landing party. A man with arms like tree trunks and a face so rough he looks unfinished. "You need help?" he asks. "What are you doing here?"

"Take me to the cliff," says Scarlett. "Tell me what's happening."

Arthur takes her arm and leads her across the churchyard. She feels the wind rush up from the sea and lash her hair about her cheeks. They are close to the edge of the cliff.

"No sign of your brother's ship yet," says Arthur.

"Is he to land on the eastern beach? Use the tunnel?"

"Ayes. We'll make our way down there when we see the

ship." For several moments he says nothing. Then his gravelly voice makes Scarlett start. "There's a light at the edge of the bay. The revenue men are watching."

Asher huddles at the end of the tunnel, listening for any sounds from the cellar. He hears nothing. If Caroline and the witch are speaking, their voices are being swallowed by the rock.

He had tried to warn her. Pick to rock and this would no longer be their secret. He had not been surprised to hear the witch's footsteps. Just surprised it had taken her so long to find them.

At the sound of footsteps, Asher had grabbed Caroline's arm and tried to pull her into the tunnel. She yanked away. She had to find the money, she told him. Had to save Mary. It didn't matter if Flora found them.

Asher looked back at the gaping hole they had made beside the tunnel entrance. There was an empty space behind the bricks. A perfect hiding place. But it was shatteringly, sickeningly empty. "The money's not here," he said. "Jacob lied to you."

"No. It must be here. It must be. I have to find it."

Asher looked at the dust and splintered brick scattered around his feet.

There was no money. Caroline was just blind with desperation.

Jacob had been playing with them both. Punishment for all they had done to him. And yet Asher had not seen it. He had been mad enough to try and believe again.

The witch's footsteps were coming closer.

He would not let himself be seen here. Couldn't bear for anyone to know he had been so foolish as to trust the ravings of Jacob Bailey.

He grabbed Caroline's hand again. "We need to leave."

She glared fiercely. "Do as you wish. I don't care." Such coldness in her eyes, her words.

And for the first time in days, Asher saw with clarity. Saw he could not pretend any longer. He was nothing to her. Never would be. Perhaps he never had been.

What hope did they have of a future?

And so he turned. Began to walk back through the tunnel. Let Caroline try and explain herself when the witch found her in the cellar with bricks around her feet. Let her admit she had fallen for Jacob's lies.

He can feel cold threads of air sighing in from the beach. His boots sink into the sand as he breaks through the mouth of the tunnel and trudges towards the sea. He will not stay here and be reminded that he had fallen again for the myth of Avery's haul. Will not be reminded that his love is unrequited.

He sees the lights of a ship at the edge of the bay. Too large to be Isaac Bailey's lugger. A revenue cutter perhaps? It is close enough to row out to.

To hell with Avery's money. There are other ways to make his fortune. He will approach the revenue vessel and tell Customs all they want to know. Reward money in exchange for his knowledge. An anonymous informant, of course.

With a swell of fresh determination, Asher shoves the dory into the sea.

"I see the lugger," Ned Arthur reports. "Coming around the point."

Scarlett's heart begins to thunder. She knows Isaac would not be returning without Mary. Dare she hope for good news? "Where is the revenue ship?"

"On the edge of the bay."

Isaac will be prepared for this, Scarlett tells herself. Customs have been watching the harbour for weeks. There is no element of surprise to their attack. The lugger is faster, and Isaac has been outrunning revenue men for almost half his life. Still, their presence makes her uneasy.

She hears the distant clatter of hooves. "Who's there?" she whispers. "Riding officers?"

"I don't know." Arthur's voice is close to her ear. "It's too dark to tell."

The sound of hooves comes closer. Drumming, echoing, approaching the bell house from the top of Bridles Lane. Scarlett hears movement around her; footsteps sighing through the grass. How many of the landing party are here in the cemetery?

"We've got to hide," Arthur hisses.

He begins to run through the churchyard, tugging Scarlett along behind him. She stumbles awkwardly, disoriented by the sudden movement.

And she loses her grip on his arm. Has he pulled away or has she let go on her own accord, aware she is slowing him down? She cannot be sure. She only knows she is alone.

The sound of hooves has stopped. Are the riding officers here, prowling through the churchyard?

She knows she cannot speak, cannot call out, in case someone should hear her. She takes a long breath to steady herself. She reaches around her, trying to place herself within the churchyard. She has seen the place almost every day of her life. And yet fear is blurring the details. Her fingers graze the tops of gravestones. They are far too small to hide behind.

Somewhere in the distance, she can hear footsteps sighing through the wet grass. Do they belong to the landing party or the riding officers?

She needs to make for the church. She knows the revenue men will not hesitate to search it— they have had their eyes on the place since the night of Bobby Carter's death— but there will be places inside she can hide. Behind the pulpit, under the pews, beneath the table in the vicar's vestry.

She trails a hand over the graves until she finds the path. She follows it towards the church and pushes on the heavy door. It opens with a groan.

Inside smells of incense and candle wax. A familiar scent of funerals and marriages and sleep-deprived Sundays. She knows this building. She can find her way.

She edges towards the pulpit and crouches in the dark.

BURNING LIGHT

The church door creaks open. Scarlett holds her breath and presses her back hard against the pulpit. She hears footsteps. Two men. Perhaps three.

Sharp, clean footsteps. Riding officers' boots.

She has no thought of how dark it is. She can smell the waxy trail of extinguished candles, but if there is even one flame left burning, if there is even a thread of moonlight shafting over her face, it could lead the riding officers straight to her.

She presses her eyes against her knees, trying to keep her face hidden. Trying to let her dark hair cloak her.

The footsteps come closer. Scarlett presses a hand against her mouth to silence her noisy breathing.

Closer they come. Closer still.

And then more distant. The door creaks open and the footsteps fade. The clop of hooves vanishes up the lane.

She knows the revenue men will not go far. They will

prowl Bridles Lane, watching the beaches, waiting for their chance to catch the Talland smugglers with their hands full of French wine.

Scarlett stands shakily, gripping the edge of the pulpit to keep her balance. She feels her way to the door of the church and heaves it open. Cold air blows against her cheeks.

"Mr Arthur?" Her whisper is swallowed quickly by the night. She waits.

Silence.

Has the landing party dispersed? Scarlett can't be sure. But if they truly have left, there will be no one to alert Isaac of the riding officers' presence. No one to warn him not to land in Talland.

She needs to find the signalling lantern. Needs to find a bundle of furze to set alight.

She makes her way outside.

A headstone, another, another. And then the row of graves stops. Ahead of her, Scarlett knows, is the thin strip of earth on which she has stood so many times with a signalling lamp. Beyond that; cliffs and sea.

She feels for the headstone at the furthest end of the churchyard. It belongs to Elizabeth Hodge, Martha Francis's mother. Behind it, the lantern is hidden. Scarlett reaches down, letting out her breath in relief as her fingers touch the cold metal. Beside it sits the tinderbox and a bundle of dried furze. The riding officers had not found it.

Slowly, she begins to walk towards the cliff edge. Each footstep is slow and tentative, testing the ground ahead of her before she edges forward.

The darkness seems to be moving, shifting, rolling like sea. She kneels dizzily. Finds the ground solid beneath her.

She strikes the tinderbox. And there is light.

A flicker, a pin prick, piercing the darkness. But it is enough to steal the air from her lungs.

The blackness returns. Hurriedly, she strikes the flint again. The charcloth flares. Yes, light. Bigger this time, bolder. Orange and yellow and hot in front of her eyes. The beauty of it makes her cry out.

She holds up the tinderbox with shaking hands. She sees nothing but the erratic dance of the flame, but right now, that flame is enough. She lights the dried fronds of the furze.

And she sees more; sees white peaks as the sea breaks against the cliff, sees the inky shape of the church. Sees the jagged stone teeth of the graves, their images blurring and sharpening.

She holds up the burning furze towards the dark shape of the lugger. This path is not safe, the flame tells her brother. The riding officers are watching.

Scarlett stamps out the furze as it burns down towards her fingers. With the fire out, the darkness has returned and she can see little.

She panics. Have her eyes failed her again, or is this just the thickness of the night? She holds the tinderbox to the wick of the lamp, exhaling in relief as shapes appear out of the darkness.

Isaac will take the lugger to Polperro. He will slip the tubs into the sea and land his most precious of cargoes. She needs to be there. Needs to help him find a safe path, away from the riding officers' eyes.

With the mast lamp doused, the lugger is suspended in

blackness. But every curve and crag of these cliffs is familiar. The pale moonlight is enough to show Isaac the way.

His skin is hot, despite the bitter cold. His heart has not slowed since they had left Leach's cutter.

Now the children are safe, they must try and escape again. They have little money, but somehow they will find a way. There is no other option. Leach will come for his family, for certain. He will come for retribution, for that phantom silver. But he will not be foolish enough to come tonight, Isaac is sure, not with the revenue men circling like sharks.

Isaac had not been surprised to see the customs ship patrolling the entrance of the bay. No doubt they have been watching the harbour. Have been waiting patiently for his return.

A flame on the cliffs in Talland. He cannot land on the eastern beach as planned. He will have to make for Polperro. Slide the lugger between the shards of cliff and land around the point.

He is prepared for this, he reminds himself. He has landed in Polperro many times. And he knows the lugger well enough to outrun the revenue men. But never before has he tried such a thing with his daughter sleeping below deck.

He sees another shape riding the inky sea. A dory, moving steadily towards the customs ship. Isaac squints. He can't make out who is aboard. He turns to Will, who is standing at the wheel.

"The spying glass." He holds it to his eye. There is just one man in the dory. Isaac feels a faint flicker of relief. The revenue men, he knows, never work alone. He looks back through the glass. In the darkness the figure is hazy, but familiar. This is Asher Hales.

Isaac's fist clenches around the neck of the spying glass.

His relief disappears.

Hales is heading straight for the revenue cutter.

The bastard has done his best to expose the Talland ring. Has sent the revenue men after them before. No doubt he is seeking to do the same thing now.

"Come about," Isaac hisses to Will. "We need to catch him."

Asher Hales knows far too many of their secrets to let him climb aboard that ship.

Scarlett's steps are unsteady on the cliff path. It feels as though her eyes are remembering how to see. She walks as far from the edge as possible, her fingers clutching the heather on the rim of the path to keep her afloat. Her other hand is tight around the handle of the unlit lantern.

She hurries towards the harbour, the steep path pulling her into a run. She will make for the point on the other side of the village. Signal to Isaac from there.

But there is Jamie, standing at the edge of the anchorage, his eyes following the light of the revenue cutter as it moves across the water.

Look at him with his messy waves of hair and his worn broadcloth coat. Look at the fine curve of his chin and the ropey muscles in his hands. He is everything she remembers.

She flings her arms around his neck.

"You see me," he says into her hair. The lantern bumps against his side. He steps back. Eyes it.

She sees him. And what does he see?

He has seen her running over the clifftops with a signalling lantern in her hand. No doubt he has seen the riding officers charging through the village. That's why he is here at the harbour, Scarlett is sure. To see if these traders will entrap themselves in the revenue men's net.

Does he wish for such a thing to happen?

This man, with his riding officer's journal and his brass buttoned coat, has a hatred for smuggling.

I despise it because it's wrong, he'd told her. *Dishonest and wrong.*

If he watches her signal from the clifftops, how long will it be before he despises her too?

"Go back to the inn," she says. "Please."

"Go back to the inn?" he repeats. "And hide away from all that's happening?" His voice is calm and even as always, but Scarlett hears a hint of tension beneath.

"Please," she says, her voice wavering. "Isaac has Mary. I need to help him get ashore." She lowers her eyes. "And I don't want you to see the things I do."

Isaac grips the gunwale. They are close to the revenue ship. Far too close. But they need to reach Asher's dory. They cannot let the bastard get aboard the cutter. Out will come their secrets, and everything will fall. Hales will implicate Scarlett, will implicate Flora. Customs will find Will on the lugger and the landing party on the beach. Isaac knows he will not be the only one to face the court.

He eases the lugger towards the dory, cutting across the path of the revenue cutter.

A bullet flies over their bow. They are in range of the

customs ship.

And from this, Isaac knows there will be only one outcome. The lugger will be captured.

This knowledge brings a strange sense of calm. He wants Reuben's ship to be caught, Isaac realises. He wants this lugger, with smuggled liquor hidden its bulkheads, to fall into the hands of the revenue men. Wants the ship to be torn apart, wants her pieces to be sold at auction.

Isaac looks down at Asher's boat. They are close. If they launched their own dory, he and Will could row out to meet him.

And so he fills their lifeboat with mooring ropes and spare balls and powder. Fills it with the things he will need to make Asher Hales compliant.

He runs below deck for Mary. He has strapped her to the mattress with a mooring rope to stop her crawling from the bunk. Is glad she has managed to sleep through the whole ordeal. He pulls her free of the rope. Slips off his coat and wraps her in its bulk.

He climbs back onto deck and helps Will wind the davits, lowering the dory into the sea. And down the ladder towards the lifeboat he climbs, leaving the ship that has been in his care for more than fourteen years. What a joy it is to abandon her here, in the path of the revenue men.

Will takes the oars and pulls away from the lugger, hidden by the thick of the night. Isaac glances edgily across the sea. The revenue cutter to his left. Asher Hales to his right. He has his pistol in one hand, his daughter in the other.

Never again, he thinks. When all this is over, his children will never see him with a weapon again.

Asher has seen them coming. He has changed course. Away from the revenue men, towards the open water.

Isaac lifts his gun. "Stop."

At the sight of the pistol, Asher stops rowing. Isaac smiles wryly to himself.

Coward.

Will lifts the oars and lets their gunwale collide with Asher's The two boats groan and thud against each other. Will and Isaac climb into Asher's dory. They yank him to his feet, making the boat tilt wildly. Water spills over the gunwale.

Isaac keeps his gun steady. For not the first time that night, he wishes he had it in him to pull the trigger. Asher Hales no longer in their lives is an enticing prospect.

Will binds Asher's wrists with mooring rope and shoves him to his knees. "What will we do with him?"

They cannot let him go. He knows too much.

Perhaps they can imprison him in Flora's cellar. Bind his wrists and ankles so he has no chance of escape. No chance of turning them in.

Isaac looks over his shoulder at the drifting lugger. When Reuben discovers his ship has been captured, he will be at the cottage door, of course. Demanding an explanation. Demanding repayment.

It doesn't matter. Isaac has his children. Once the revenue men have turned their backs, he and his family will find a way to leave.

He watches the lugger career across the path of the customs vessel.

Let them catch her. Let them think her a ghost ship.

Go back to the inn, Scarlett had said. Jamie feels hot and restless. He wishes he were able to do as she had asked. Wishes he were able to turn away from all that is unfolding. But he needs to watch. He is as ingrained in this world as Scarlett is.

He stands outside the inn and looks over the water. The two ships are close together. But there is something strange about the way the lugger is moving; a drunken dance, her sails limp and windless.

There is no one aboard. Jamie is sure of it. Isaac has left the ship to fall into the hands of the authorities. A deliberate act, no doubt. Has he escaped in their lifeboat? Does he have his daughter?

Jamie can just make out Scarlett's tiny figure at the top of the cliff.

She has seen the strange motion of the lugger, he is sure. She will know her brother is no longer aboard. Will know he is trying to land.

She has set a light flickering on the point. What is she telling Isaac? Jamie rubs his eyes. How many nights has he spent squinting into the dark, trying to determine the language of lanterns on the cliffs?

Whatever the meaning, it doesn't matter. Scarlett is not safe. She is hidden from the revenue men riding the roads of Talland, but has made herself a beacon for those who will be coming from the west. The riding officers will have banded together to hem in the pocket of coast they suspect is seeing action.

Scarlett must know this, surely. She has spent her life outrunning the revenue men. But she is acting rashly, desperate to get her brother, her niece, safely ashore.

Hell. She will trap herself up there.

Her brother will land safely, but the riding officers will

take her instead.

Jamie curses under his breath. He had promised her he would not involve himself in her corner of the trade. But it is far too late for that.

He runs into the inn and snatches the saddle bag holding his pistol and powder. Hurries to the stables for his horse.

REVENUE MEN

Jamie rides towards the lantern Scarlett has set flickering on the cliff.

He cannot see her in the pale orange light. There is nothing around but coarse scrub and she has hidden herself well. She is sickeningly good at this.

"Scarlett," he hisses.

She appears from behind him. He cannot even tell where she had been hiding.

Her eyes are wide. "Why are you—"

"Get on the horse," Jamie hisses. "Now."

She moves to douse the lantern, but he yanks her away. "Leave it burning. Let the officers come this way." He grabs her arm and pulls her into the saddle behind him.

Inky plains of farmland stretch out ahead. Beyond that? He has no thought. But they cannot ride the path. Officers will be approaching from either side, drawn to the signal fire on top of the cliff.

He digs his heels in, goading the horse into a gallop.

Scarlett's arms tighten around him.

Hooves thunder across the farmland, the horse leaping the thin threads of the streams. Jamie's heart is thundering. His cheeks burn in the cold air. He dares a glance over his shoulder. He hears hoof falls, fast and rhythmic. They are growing steadily louder.

Had they seen Scarlett on the cliff? Would they recognise her if they were to find her on the back of his horse?

He hears her sharp intake of breath beside his ear. Her arms tighten around his waist.

"Let me off," she says breathlessly. "Let them catch me. They can't see you with me. They'll find out who you are. You'll lose everything."

Jamie keeps riding.

He knows she is right. If he is found in league with these smugglers he will have nothing to return home to but a prison cell. There is too much corruption in the revenue service for the courts to make light of it.

He pushes the thought away.

Ahead of them, the farmland gives way to trees and tangled scrub. The branches are too low-hanging to ride through. He skirts the edge of the woodland, cutting into the trees as they thin slightly. Moonlight shafts through the bare branches.

When they break into the open again, the lights of a village are flickering ahead of them. Jamie slows the horse to a walk. "Where are we?"

"We're in Killigarth." Scarlett's breath is hot and fast against his ear. "Do you think we lost them?"

Jamie listens. He hears the murmur of a stream. Hears soft, distant footsteps. He hears no horses. "I think so."

"I've got to get back to Polperro," says Scarlett. "I've got to help Isaac." She points to a narrow path snaking up the incline. "That's Talland Hill. It will take us back to the village."

Jamie tugs on the reins and begins the descent. The road is narrow and slippery. Clouds billow across the moon.

And here comes the thunder of hooves again. Talland Hill, Jamie realises, will lead them into the village, but it will also lead them into the revenue men's path.

"Hide," he hisses. "I'll draw them away."

Scarlett leaps from the horse and buries herself in the undergrowth.

Jamie rides back up the hill towards Killigarth. He fires his pistol. The sound splinters the cold night, eliciting a screech from somewhere in the village. He reaches into his saddle bag and pulls out his riding officer's jacket, along with his peasant knife.

He flicks open the blade and swipes it across his palm. Lets the blood run over the white trimming on the edges of the coat. He climbs from the horse and tramples the jacket into the dirt. Reloads the pistol. Another shot to bring the riding officers closer.

He waves them down. "You've men patrolling out here?"

The officer nods. "We do."

Jamie holds out the jacket. "I found this on the road. Looks as though a man has been injured."

The officer takes the coat, inspects the bloodstains. "Where did you find this?"

Jamie points towards the hills, away from Scarlett, away from her brother's landing. He keeps his other hand hidden behind his back, a seam of blood trickling between his fingers and spilling onto the earth.

The dory grinds through the shallow water, thudding against the rock. They are hidden from the revenue men by a dark curtain of cliff. From here, they can climb ashore and wade around the point to the beach.

Isaac glances up at the clifftop. The signal flame has disappeared, leaving only starlight above them. He holds Mary tightly and climbs from the boat, leaving the dory to be carried away on the tide.

Will shoves his pistol into Asher's back, forcing him to walk. His hands are tightly bound behind him.

"Make a sound," Will hisses, "and I'll shoot you."

Asher snorts. "And what fate do you have in store for me if I remain quiet? Something similar, I assume."

They wind their way past the harbour and up onto the cliffs. Mary is wide-eyed and alert, peeking out from beneath the folds of Isaac's coat. She follows the men with a sharp gaze that is more than a little Caroline.

As they wind their way onto the cliffs, Isaac says: "You helped Tom Leach take my children. Why?"

Asher doesn't look at him. "I helped your son escape. I risked my life for him."

Isaac pushes past his excuses. "What have I done to you that's so damn terrible?"

Asher snorts. "It's not about you."

And here is that unsteadying hot-then-coldness. Isaac thinks of Leach's words.

Your daughter for the silver your wife knows how to find.

He tries to force the thought from his mind. Leach is a madman. A liar. Asher Hales is little better. And yet he finds himself asking:

"Is it about my wife? And this haul of silver?"

"There is no silver," Asher says bitterly.

Isaac grits his teeth. "What of Caroline? Does this involve her?"

Asher gives a cold laugh. "Why are you asking me? Why not ask your wife? Or your father?"

Isaac feels the words cut into him. He does not look back at Asher. Cannot let him see the uncertainty in his face. Cannot let him see the way his words have rattled him. He lifts Mary higher onto his shoulder. To hell with Hales, with Leach, with their lies. He will not walk into these traps they are laying. He has far more important things to concern himself with.

"Take Hales to the Mariner's Arms," he tells Will. "Tell Flora all that's happened." He glances down at the baby. "I've got to get Mary home."

SPLINTERING

Caroline cannot bear this waiting. The night is so still she can hear the sea sighing against the beach. Can hear Gabriel breathing through his closed bedroom door. Hears drops of old rain plinking from the roof.

She glances at the fish kettle in which she has hidden the silver. No one will find it there. Not even her husband.

If Isaac has not returned in two days' time, she will take the money to The Ship and give it to Tom Leach. And she will spend her life wondering whether Flora Kelly feels guilty enough to keep silent. There is something bitterly cruel about it, Caroline thinks. Having her most destructive secrets in the hands of the woman who had lain with her husband.

But then there are footsteps. The creak of the door. And there is Isaac with their daughter in his arms.

Caroline cries out, rushes to them. She snatches Mary, holds her tight, tighter, against her thumping chest.

She throws an arm around Isaac, pulls him into her, her arm latched around his neck. His hand slides to the small of

196

her back. It is an habitual gesture, but there is no warmth to it. Caroline feels something tighten in her stomach.

It doesn't matter. Mary is here, safe, bright-eyed. Pawing at her mother's neckerchief and speaking indecipherable words.

Caroline sinks to the floor beside the hearth. She can't get her daughter close enough. Finally, she looks up at Isaac. Tears are blurring her vision. "Where did you find her?"

"On the river."

"Does Leach know you have her?"

He nods.

Caroline's eyes drift to the fish kettle. They have their children. They have the silver. And she has a story concocted that will place the blame at Asher's feet. It will be easy enough for Isaac to believe. After all, Asher Hales had been one of the men who had taken their children.

They have their chance. They must take it now, before any of the people holding her secrets see fit to open their mouth. She reaches up for Isaac's hand. "Let's leave," she says. "Right now."

"We can't leave tonight. Customs are about. They've seized Reuben's lugger. They'll be expecting me to run. If they catch us on the road, they'll see it as an admission of guilt."

There is coldness in his voice. Caroline's chest tightens. What does he know? Has Scarlett spilled the news about their father? Told Isaac of how Asher had been whispering to his wife in the street?

Caroline climbs to her feet. She pulls Isaac close, Mary squeezed between them. Perhaps if she holds him tight enough, wishes hard enough, she will take things back to that secretive, sheltered place they had been before Asher Hales had washed up upon their shore.

Mary and Gabriel are safe. How desperately she had longed for this. Just for now, let her curl up beside her family, with her husband and children in her arms. Just for now. Before everything crumbles.

She stands close to Isaac, trying to inhale every breath of him. She presses a hand to his arm, memorising the feel of him beneath her. Just for now. Let them lie in the dark together and let his coldness fade away.

"You need to rest," she tells him. "You've not slept properly in days." She brushes the hair from his face. Looks into his eyes. She cannot read him. For the first time in their marriage, he feels like a stranger.

After a moment, he takes a step back. "Go to bed," he says stiffly. "I'll wait up a while. Make sure there's no trouble."

Scarlett waits by the door of the stables. She hears Jamie's footsteps inside, hears a metallic rattle as he returns the saddle to its hook.

Her chest aches. She cannot bear to face him.

Finally, he steps outside. Scarlett takes his hand in both of hers. In the flickering light of the lamp above the door, she can see the neckcloth knotted around his palm. Sees the specks of crimson beneath.

"You need to leave," she says, her voice coming out as little more than a whisper. "I'll not have you dragged down by me."

For a long time, Jamie doesn't speak. Doesn't look at her. "Why did you have to get involved in this life?" he asks finally.

Scarlett swallows the pain in her throat. It is a question for Jacob, not for her. She has never had a choice. But this does not feel like a time for excuses.

How desperately she wants to turn her back on this world. How desperately she wants to ride back to Portreath with Jamie's arms around her and live a life without Charles Reuben in it.

Tears prick her eyes and she blinks them away hurriedly. "I can't leave my family," she manages. "I can't leave Isaac to carry our father's debts alone."

"I know," Jamie says softly. "I know."

He pulls her into him. Holds her wordlessly for a long time. Scarlett keeps her arms clamped around his waist. She presses her head into his neck.

She can't bring herself to let go. Because when she does, it will be the end. Jamie deserves far better than her.

Finally, he steps back. "I want to stay until I know your family is safe," he says. "If Isaac has Mary, Leach is bound to retaliate."

"No," Scarlett says firmly. "You need to leave tonight. Please." She can't bear for him to be here any longer.

After a moment, he nods. "If that's what you wish."

She swallows hard, forcing her tears away.

He opens his mouth to speak.

"No," Scarlett says hurriedly. "Don't tell me goodbye. I couldn't bear it."

Jamie draws in his breath. Nods wordlessly and steps back into the stables.

And Scarlett puts her head down and walks, unable to watch him go.

DEBTS

Scarlett sits on the point, listening the sea clop against the rock. She shivers violently. Tugs her cloak tighter around her body.

She wishes she could feel joy. Gabriel and Mary are safe. She can see the world around her again. But it does not push aside the ache deep within her.

A part of her has always known she and Jamie was an impossibility. She had tried to convince herself otherwise, tried to believe their feelings for each other were enough to overcome their differences. But they are firmly planted on opposite sides of the law. Being with her will only bring him down.

She feels watched. For a moment she is afraid to turn around. Who is there? Leach? Reuben? The authorities? But no. It is her father watching her from the edge of the beach. He steps carefully across the rocks and sits at her side. Scarlett shifts uncomfortably.

"You see me," he says.

She nods. Turns away so he can't catch her eye.

"I watched the ships come in," he says. "What's happened? Is Isaac safe?"

Scarlett nods. "Ayes. And so are the children."

And out come the obligatory responses. I'm so glad, thank the Lord, tonight we can sleep... Things Jacob Bailey, who had abandoned his children, has no right to say. Scarlett grits her teeth, swallowing her anger.

"What will you do?" he asks.

She hugs her knees. "I don't know. If we try to leave this place again, Reuben's men will be watching. I don't know if we can take that risk." She looks squarely at her father. This is his chance, she thinks. If he wants to earn his way back into their lives, this is it. This is his opportunity to go to Reuben, show him he is alive. Tell him the debt belongs to him and not to his son.

Jacob doesn't speak. Just nods slowly. "Reuben is a dangerous man," he says. And then no more. Nothing to suggest he might do as Scarlett had hoped. Nothing to suggest he might be willing to shoulder the debt that is rightfully his. The back of her neck prickles with anger.

"Please leave," she says shortly. "I don't want you here." She turns away, making it clear the conversation is over.

Jacob stands. On the edge of her vision, Scarlett sees him nod. And then he is gone.

Finally, she climbs to her feet. She trudges across the beach, chased by the edge of the tide.

As she makes her way back into the village, she sees her father walking alone through the empty street. His chin is lifted, and his steps are long and fast. He climbs the hill towards Reuben's house.

Scarlett finds herself following.

Jacob slides through the gate and makes his way to the

back of the property, hidden in the shadow of the house. He weaves through the dark garden and finds the door leading to the servants' quarters. He reaches into his pocket. Pulls out, what? A tool? Scarlett cannot make it out. Jacob shoves it into the lock and wrenches until the door pops open. He disappears inside.

Scarlett runs across the grass and slips into the house. She follows the servants' passage past rows of rough-hewn wooden doors, some with rhythmic snores coming from behind them. She passes the kitchen with its lingering scent of roast meat, passes the laundry that smells of wet clothes.

The door leading up to the mansion is hanging open. Scarlett climbs the stairs. And she is in Reuben's lavish entrance hall. She has not been inside since she was a child. The house is bathed in darkness, lit only by the moon pushing through the curtains. She can make out the inky shape of the grand staircase, the spidery arms of the brass chandelier. There is a strange familiarity to it, as though it has been days since she had last been inside, rather than years.

Jacob, it seems, also remembers the place well. Scarlett can see his figure at the top of the stairs. He disappears into the passage towards what she guesses are bedrooms.

Scarlett begins to climb.

At the top of the staircase she looks about her. The passage stretches out in either direction, the hall thick with the lingering scent of melted wax.

A creak of the floorboards to her left. The door to one of the bedchambers hangs open a crack. Scarlett creeps down the passage and peeks into the room. Reuben is lying on his back on a wide, curtained bed, breathing deeply in sleep. Jacob stands at his bedside, a knife in his hand.

Scarlett holds her breath, unable to move.

She watches as Jacob presses his blade into Reuben's neck. Why does she say nothing? Why is she simply letting this happen? Blood fountains from the wound, black in the faint light. Scarlett watches it run over Reuben's shoulder and pool on the floor.

She cannot tell if he wakes. Does he see the face of his killer? Or does he slip away from this life without so much as an exhalation?

Scarlett covers her mouth, feeling her own cry well up from her throat. She had known, before this, that her father had killed. Countless times, she had pictured him on the landing beach, pulling the trigger on Albert Davey. And yet it had remained a distant, intangible thing.

There is no distance to this. Nothing intangible. This is far too real. For all the gratitude she has for the return of her sight, Scarlett wishes she had not had to witness this.

She wants him to know. Wants him to know that she is here, and she has seen.

She steps into the room. Jacob is standing over the body, staring at the silky pool of blood, as though he is afraid Reuben might be suddenly resurrected.

Scarlett takes another step towards the stained bed. Her heart is thumping. Reuben's eyes are glassy. She is sure she can see surprise in them.

Jacob turns. Doesn't speak at once. He glances down at the knife in his hand. "You saw me," he says.

Scarlett doesn't respond. She knows there is no need. She keeps walking, closer and closer to the body. He is gone, this man who has held her family prisoner for so much of her life. She needs to see. Needs to be certain. It doesn't feel real.

She looks down. His blood is on her boots, on the hems of her skirts.

This house is full of workers. Men and women who could wake at any time. They will find her here with a body before her and blood on her skirts.

And she will not go to the scaffold for Jacob Bailey's crimes.

She turns abruptly and hurries from the house. And as she marches through the narrow streets towards the cliff path, she realises. The murder had been carefully planned. Jacob had known what he needed to pick the lock, had known the location of the servants' entrance, had known which door had led to Reuben's bedroom.

He had been planning this, she sees, since he had arrived in Polperro. And for how long before that?

She is aware of him walking behind her. She doesn't stop. Doesn't turn.

He says: "I just wanted you and Isaac to be free of him."

"And this is how you thought to do it?"

Jacob had blamed the anger inside him for the murder of Albert Davey. The Wild had seized him and taken away all reason.

But this had not been wild anger. This had been cold-blooded and calculated. Murder for his own gain. Just as Davey's had been.

Jacob reaches for Scarlett's arm to stop her leaving. "You're free of him now. You and Isaac ought to go and live your lives. Get away from this place."

Scarlett thinks of Jamie. Thinks to tell him they are free. Thinks to tell him she has a chance to build a life without free trade in it.

And then she looks down. Sees the blood staining her skirts. Feels the Wild inside her, dormant, but waiting. And she feels her father's blood pulsing in her veins. Killer's blood.

Was it truly Reuben who had drawn her into a life of crime? Or had that tendency been lying inside her all along? Perhaps she had had no choice in the matter. Perhaps this is just who she is.

She cannot go to Jamie with blood staining her skirts. He is far too good for that. He is far too good for a wife who stands by and watches a man die.

"You ought to go back to Talland," says Jacob. "Someone will find the body soon." There is sadness in his voice, as though he knows he has lost whatever fragile chance at reconciliation he might have had.

He is right to be sad. Scarlett does not want this man in her life. Does not want this reminder of what impulses might lie inside her, coiled up beside the Wild.

But there are pieces that do not sit right.

"You told me once that everything you'd done was for me." She doesn't look at him. "What did you mean by that?"

Jacob sighs heavily. "It doesn't matter. It's too late for any of this. It's best I just go. You're far better off without me."

"The night you left you were upset. I remember you crying. Why?"

He looks at the ground for a long time. Finally, he meets her eyes. "Because I believed I was never going to see you again."

"That was your choice."

"Well." He glances back at Reuben's mansion. "We all make bad choices."

She doesn't speak.

"Go, Scarlett," he says.

She gives a faint nod. And up she walks, over the cliff. The path is lit only by the moon, but after days of darkness, it feels as bright as morning. Her steps are crooked with weariness, with emotion, with lingering flashes of dizziness.

She stumbles down the hill into Talland and lets herself into the cottage.

Isaac is asleep, sitting up against the wall. A half-burned log splinters in the gate. He opens his eyes as Scarlett stumbles towards him.

He sees it all, she realises. Sees the blood on her skirts, the anguish in her face, sees her eyes dart around the cottage as though they are taking it in for the first time.

She drops to her knees beside him. "Isaac," she says, her voice splintering, "our father is alive."

TRUTHS AND LIES

She tells him everything. Tells him of Asher's letter and the murder of Albert Davey. Tells him of Portreath; of Jacob's press gang and Jamie's brass buttons. The way the light had returned as she had stood on the cliff. And she tells him of the pool of blood that now lies at the side of Charles Reuben's bed.

Isaac listens without speaking. By the time she has finished, there are tears pouring down her face, but Scarlett feels a weight lifted from her shoulders. Isaac slides an arm around her, pulling her into him. With the two of them sitting alone in front of the fire, it feels suddenly as though she is back in her childhood; a time that has come to feel far more distant than it truly is.

"I wish you'd told me earlier," Isaac says gently. "You didn't have to carry all this alone."

His eyes are glassy, underlined with shadows of exhaustion. A faint frown creases the bridge of his nose.

"What are you thinking?" she asks.

He lets out his breath. "I don't know, Scarlett. I don't even know where to begin."

She turns to look at the stripe of dawn light pushing through the curtains. "I think he's gone back to Portreath," she says. Gone back to that cottage on the hill. Gone before men on horses come seeking Reuben's killer.

Isaac looks into the fire. He makes no effort to move, to catch sight of his father, to chase him over the hills. She has made the right decision, Scarlett thinks, in letting Jacob go.

They will have a new life outside of Talland, and their father will have no place in it.

Isaac squeezes her shoulder. "Go and change your clothes. Gabriel will be up soon and I don't want him to see the blood."

She nods, climbing to her feet and making her way to her bedroom. The stained skirts belong to Flora, she realises. The blood has soaked through the sky blue wool, blackening it in patches. Scarlett climbs out of them, kicking them into the corner of her room. She cannot bear to look at them. Can't bear to look at that bloody reminder of all her family is.

Isaac stands outside the house, the blue-grey morning lightening around him. His thoughts are tangled with exhaustion. How is he to make sense of all he has learned?

Jacob, alive. He is shocked, of course, but Scarlett's news is strangely easy to accept. His father had always been one to put himself first. One who had sought wealth with little regard for decency. For him to have saddled his children with his debts is far from implausible.

Jacob will not be waiting in Polperro for a coach. With Reuben's blood on his hands he will have little choice but to leave on foot. Get as far from the place as possible before the body is discovered.

He cannot have gotten far.

Isaac goes to the Millers' farm for the horse. Up over the clifftop he rides, watching the sun break over the horizon. He sees the lugger at the edge of the anchorage. Today the revenue men will take her to Looe for auction. The ship will be broken up, her parts sold to the highest bidder. Isaac wishes he could watch. There would be a great sense of satisfaction to seeing that ship in pieces.

He keeps riding. Out of Polperro, onto the narrow road winding northwards towards Portreath. He knows he will not be able to ride too far. Knows the revenue men will be watching.

In the pearly light, he sees a man walking alone on the road. His shoulders are hunched, his grey hair loose at his neck. He watches his feet as he walks. Isaac can only see the back of his head, but he knows the man is his father.

He stops the horse. For a moment, he considers turning around. What does he have to say to this man? Why has he come? To see for himself, he supposes.

He takes the horse closer. Jacob turns.

Isaac stares at his father. He is older, of course, but there is something achingly familiar about him. Something that tells Isaac that Jacob Bailey is the same dangerous, hard-edged man he had been sixteen years ago.

Jacob digs his hands into his pockets. It is too late. Isaac has already seen the blood staining his fingers.

"You've come to see if it were true then?" Jacob asks finally.

"Something like that." What does he really want? Why has he ridden so impulsively across the clifftops to catch sight of the father he had never wanted in his life?

Jacob sniffs. "When I left, I—"

"Don't." Isaac shakes his head. "Scarlett's already told me all I need to know."

Jacob lowers his eyes. "I see."

Isaac's hands tighten around the reins. He regrets coming. "Why return?" he asks finally. "After all this time?"

Jacob looks at the ground. "I thought perhaps I could put things right."

"Put things right? By killing Charles Reuben?"

"You'd expect no less from me, surely." There is a hint of bitterness in his voice.

"And who do you imagine they'll suspect?" asks Isaac. "Who do you suppose they'll pin the murder on? No one has a better motive for killing Reuben than me."

Jacob looks down at his ragged cloth shoes. "Take your family and leave, Isaac. Have the life you ought to have had."

Yes, he ought to leave. What is stopping him?

"Why are you really here?" Jacob asks after a moment. "Is it because you have questions for me?"

Isaac feels his muscles tighten. This, of course, is the real reason he had bolted up the hills on a borrowed horse. Because he has questions he is unable to ignore. Because the last time he had looked into his wife's eyes he had seen a stranger. He has begun to doubt the woman who has been his anchor for the past twelve years. And it feels as though the earth is shifting beneath him.

"What do you know of her?" he asks. "Caroline."

Jacob eyes him. He is looking closely. Too closely. Then he pulls his bloodstained hands from his pocket and stares down at them. After a long time, he says: "All that happened to me was my own doing. There's little point dwelling on the past."

For a second, Isaac doubts himself. He has always known his father a criminal. And now he has shown himself as so much more than a petty smuggler. He is a killer. The man who had abandoned his family. Is he really coming to this man for the truth about his wife? Is he really seeking answers to questions Tom Leach had planted in his mind? Surely he owes Caroline more than this.

"You're right," he tells Jacob. "There's little point dwelling on the past." Little point standing here with a man he has never trusted. He tugs on the reins and begins to ride back to Talland.

"Where have you been?" Caroline pushes, racing out of the cottage to meet him. Her hair has been combed and pinned neatly for the first time in days.

Isaac feels strangely reluctant to tell her any of this. Reluctant to tell her of his meeting with Jacob, or of the things he and Scarlett had spoken of that morning. What does this mean? Surely *my father is alive* is not something a man keeps from his wife.

He ignores her question. "Did the children sleep soundly?" he asks, grappling for something that might break the tense silence. The children at least, are common ground.

And Caroline is speaking, yes a part of him hears her. But he cannot fathom what she is saying. Because he sees the smugglers' banker striding up the path towards them, a pistol in his hand.

FAITHFUL MEN

Isaac hurries into the house and locks the door behind Caroline. "Take the children to the nursery. Stay close to the floor."

Scarlett appears from her bedroom. "What's happening?"

A gunshot flies through the window. Isaac feels shards of glass against his cheek. Caroline swallows a scream and slams the nursery door.

"Who is it?" Scarlett breathes hard, pressing her back against the wall.

The banker, Isaac tells her. Come to punish them for Reuben's murder.

He glances at the bedroom. He had tucked his pistol beneath the mattress when he had returned home last night.

Scarlett is closest.

"My pistol," he whispers. "Beneath the bed."

She nods silently. Disappears into the bedroom and returns with the gun. She slides it along the floor towards him.

A second shot flies through the window.

The banker is calling to them; angry garbled words. Isaac hears *coward* and *killer*. Behind the nursery door, Mary shrieks.

He squeezes the pistol. How many times has he found himself here? His life in danger and feeling unable to shoot?

Scarlett reaches for the fire poker. "Bring him inside."

Knuckles white around his gun, Isaac opens the door. He steps back to let the banker into the house.

"You killed Charles Reuben," he says, his gun held out in front of him.

This man, with his untidy grey queue and bristled chin looks just as he has for the past fourteen years. Soulless. Blank. The look of a man who acts on another's bidding.

"Do you have proof of that?" Isaac asks tautly. He takes a step backwards, drawing the banker further into the house.

"Proof?" the banker spits. "I don't need proof. Every man in this village knows you wanted Reuben out of your life."

"You're right," says Isaac. "I did."

Scarlett moves suddenly, thrashing the poker at the banker's head. He drops heavily to the floor, his gun spilling across the kitchen.

Isaac stands over him. The man's eyes flutter and his fingers curl. Isaac finds himself lifting his pistol. He has to do this. If he doesn't shoot, there will be another man after them. Another man to take his children, to shoot through his windows, to hold a debt over his family. He feels his finger shift on the trigger.

"Don't Isaac, please," Scarlett coughs. "You can't shoot him. You can't be like our father."

Isaac hesitates.

He had never wanted to be like Jacob. Had only followed

his path out of necessity.

But he has a choice now.

Are Mary and Gabriel to face each other twenty years from now, and whisper to each other, *you can't be like our father?*

He lowers the gun.

Scarlett catches his eye and gives him a faint nod. He takes the banker's gun from the floor and tucks it into his pocket.

Caroline emerges from the bedroom with Mary on her hip. She looks down at the body. "Is he—"

"He's alive," says Isaac. "And he'll not be down for much longer. We can't stay here." His thoughts are charging. Where are they to go? They have no escape plan in place. Polperro harbour is still full of revenue men, preparing the lugger for auction.

"What does he want?" Caroline's voice is thin. "Why has he come for us?"

"Reuben is dead," Isaac says shortly. "Murdered."

"Murdered? By who?"

But he is marching into the bedroom, pulling the trunk out from under the bed. Anything to avoid the question. Anything to avoid mentioning his father. "Pack your things," he tells her.

Caroline unlatches the trunk and begins to throw their clothes inside it, the baby still clamped to her side. There is a hardness in her eyes. She has done this before, of course. Has packed up their life this way, only for Tom Leach to tear the children from her arms.

"Do you think more men will come for us?" Scarlett asks from her bedroom.

Isaac goes back to the kitchen and stares down at the banker. "I suppose now we'll find out how many of Reuben's men are loyal to him." He takes the trunk from Caroline as she drags it out of the bedroom. He sets it beside the door. "We'll go to the inn," he says. "We'll be hidden there. If more of Reuben's men come looking, they'll not be able to find us."

Caroline presses her lips into a thin white line. But she nods wordlessly.

Isaac reaches beneath the mattress and pulls out the pouch of coins. They will shelter in the Mariner's Arms until nightfall. He will find someone to bring a boat to the landing beach. Perhaps they can make their way east towards Looe. Away from Tom Leach. Away from Reuben's men. Away from the authorities.

In the dark they will be invisible.

Scarlett is waiting in the kitchen. She has a bag slung over her shoulder and her cloak hooked closed. She stands over the groaning body of the banker with a knife in her hand. Isaac meets her eyes.

They have tried this before. Tried to disappear from this place, only to face the banker's pistol.

This time there will be no failing. No returning. When he steps from this cottage, he knows it will be for the last time.

Isaac ushers his family out into the street and pulls the door closed heavily. He sees Scarlett glance at the house, but he doesn't look back.

Let this place be forgotten. The memories within it are tainted.

He wants to have faith in his wife. Wants to believe there are no secrets between them. Wants to believe Tom Leach and Asher Hales are nothing more than madmen. Wants to believe his wife has never set eyes on his father. But the doubt has been planted. It is there, undeniable, crawling beneath his skin. And it has discoloured the memories of the life they have shared.

He tucks the trunk beneath his arm and presses a hand to Gabriel's shoulder, pulling him close in an attempt to reassure him. They wind their way down the road until they reach the Mariner's Arms. Isaac pounds on the door.

"We need to hide."

Flora doesn't ask questions. She hurries them inside, locking the door after them. Above their heads, the watch ball sways in the draught. Through the silent tavern they walk, climbing the stairs to the parlour.

And they wait for the dark.

TRUST

Asher sits in the cellar with his back against the bottom step. His wrists are bound. Ankles bound. What a sorry creature he is.

Again he is a prisoner here in this dank, miserable place. The realisation is a brutal one.

This time, the tunnel is open; a black mouth vanishing into the rock. A second hole gapes beside it. In the lamplight, he sees the cavity Caroline had discovered behind the bricks. A fine place for hiding silver. And an even finer place for a lie.

Asher stares at the broken wall for a long time.

He knows for certain things won't work out the way they had the last time he was cowering down here, a shipwrecked sailor with mystery around him. Scarlett Bailey will not walk down the stairs with a wash bowl and razor in her hands and lovingly sponge away the filth. She will not primp and preen him and stare lovingly into his eyes.

No. Asher Hales is quite certain he will not leave this place alive.

Flora slips back inside the inn. She has made arrangements. At nightfall, Will Francis will be waiting on the beach, ready to steal Isaac and his family away from Talland.

She stands for a moment in the empty bar, reluctant to go upstairs and face Caroline. Reluctant to tell Isaac that tonight he will leave. It can be the only way, of course. But the thought of him disappearing is an ache inside her.

Dust dances in the faint streaks of sunlight. Glasses are lined up along the shelves, logs piled beside the cold hearth. Everything smells of beeswax polish.

Tomorrow night she will reopen the inn. Tomorrow night, when Isaac is gone. She will have something to put her mind to. A part of her longs to see the tavern's doors unlocked again.

But beneath her feet is Asher Hales. He cannot be released. He will run to the revenue men and lead them to the tunnel. Customs will be at her door within the hour.

What is she to do? Keep him a prisoner in her cellar forever? No. How can she run a tavern with a man tied up beneath her patrons' feet?

He cannot remain a prisoner indefinitely. Nor can he be released. Though she has done her best not to think of it, Flora knows the truth.

To avoid facing the courts, one of them must kill Asher Hales.

She makes her way upstairs and clicks open the door of the parlour. The room is grey and thick with shadow; the curtains pulled closed to keep out prying eyes. The logs in the grate sit cold, no smoke rising from the chimney. Perhaps no one is watching the inn, but a seemingly empty building will raise less suspicion.

Gabriel and Bessie are on their knees by the hearth, attempting to throw knucklebones in a gauntlet of dog's paws and Mary's curious fingers.

Flora can't look at Caroline, perched on the edge of the couch, gnawing her thumbnail. Can't look at Isaac, pacing by the covered window. And so she looks at Scarlett. "The boat will be ready at nightfall," she says. "Will Francis will be waiting on the eastern beach."

"Thank you." Isaac pulls the curtain back an inch and peers through the window. "Any sign of the banker? Or any of Reuben's footmen?"

Flora shakes her head. "Not that I could tell."

"Good."

"The banker saw us leave the cottage," says Scarlett, picking listlessly at the waxy candleholder on the mantle. "He'll be watching. Waiting."

Isaac nods. "With luck he'll think we've already left."

Flora leaves them in the parlour and goes to Jack's room. She runs a finger over the mallow fronds hanging across the mantle. They are not completely dry, but she needs something to put her mind to. She carefully unthreads the stems and sets them on the table. She will crush and jar them, then mix with lard for bruising.

She hears the floor creak. She knows instinctively that Isaac is behind her. Can sense him, feel him. For a moment, she is afraid to turn around.

219

"I saw the damage to the cellar wall when I went to check on Hales," he says after a moment. "What happened?"

Flora keeps her back to him. She keeps unthreading the leaves. What had happened to the cellar wall, she feels certain, is a secret that would see Caroline and Isaac's marriage torn apart. It is not her secret to tell.

However much she might wish to.

She feels his hands on her; firm against her shoulders. He is close. Too close. His breath is hot against her ear, his voice resonating within her.

"Flora," he says, "please tell me."

No. It is not her place.

"Look at me," he says.

And like an obedient child, she does, turning to look up at him, his nose inches from hers. In his eyes she sees distress, sees anxiety, sees questions.

"Was Caroline involved?" he presses. "Did she come here looking for something?"

Flora closes her eyes.

"Did she come looking for money? For Henry Avery's silver?"

"Caroline is in the next room," Flora says finally. "Why are you asking me these things? Why not ask her?"

Isaac doesn't answer at once. His fingers tighten around her shoulders, then work their way downwards until they reach the bare skin on her forearms.

"Because I trust you," he says after a moment. "And I don't trust her."

Flora forces herself away. Forces herself to ignore the tug of desire that gathers at the feel of his skin against hers. Never mind who Isaac trusts and distrusts. Come tonight he will be gone.

I trust you. And I don't trust her.

He had intended for her to hear this, Caroline has no doubt. Had heard her in the hallway, perhaps. Had known she would follow him as he trailed Flora like a doting pet.

Isaac steps from the guestroom, finding her in the passage. Yes, she has seen. Yes, she has heard. Her husband has no trust in her because he knows she was the one who had gone searching for Avery's haul. He knows she has been keeping secrets.

Caroline feels herself beginning to tremble. This is it, she realises. This is the moment she has been dreading since she had first learned who Isaac's father was. This is the moment she hovers on the edge of the cliff and struggles to pull herself back. This is the moment she can no longer outrun her past.

Jacob Bailey has won. They have reached the scenario he had engineered when he'd told her to go treasure hunting in the walls of the Mariner's Arms. The wealth unearthed. Isaac asking questions. She, with nowhere to turn but outworn lies. This is everything Jacob wants.

I trust you. And I don't trust her.

Isaac returns to the parlour without a word. He too is dreading the confrontation, Caroline can tell. He is dreading the truth he is edging closer and closer to. The truth of who his wife is and what she has done.

He leaves the door ajar. Caroline cannot bring herself to look through it. She can't look at any of them; not Mary chewing on her rag doll, or Gabriel chasing the dog. Not her husband who has learned she cannot be trusted. If she looks at any of them, she will not go.

She doesn't look at the coats slung over the back of the chairs or the knucklebones scattered across the floor or anything that might remind her of the life she had once had.

She goes to the guestroom, where Flora is untying the piece of twine hanging from the mantle. She does not let herself think. Does not let the tears that are tightening her throat become anything more than a faint pain. She closes the door behind her.

Flora looks up in surprise. Her lips part. Is she to speak? Is she to cobble together some miserable apology for breathing down the neck of another woman's husband?

Caroline couldn't bear it. She reaches into her pocket and hands her the pouch of silver she had taken from the kettle that morning. "Take it. Help my family get away."

Flora stares at the money. "What?"

Caroline grits her teeth. Must she spell things out?

Her secrets are far too close to the surface. Stay here in Talland and they will spill. The decision is brutal, but it has been made. There are things that Isaac can never know. Things her children cannot know. She would rather be alone than have her family learn who she truly is.

"I need to leave," she tells Flora. "And so do you." She keeps her eyes down. "If Tom Leach learns the money is in your inn he will come looking."

"Tom Leach won't come to this place," says Flora. "He's too afraid."

Caroline gives a cold, humourless laugh. "Do you truly believe that? There was a fortune hidden in your walls."

"Then give it to him." Flora holds out the pouch. "As you planned to do before Mary was rescued. Keep him out of our lives."

No. Isaac and the children must use this money to leave Talland. They must disappear before Jacob finds them and tells them the truth of why he left. Isaac has doubts and suspicions, but doubt is far better than knowing for certain the things his wife has done.

"I don't want Leach to have the money," she tells Flora sharply. "I want Isaac to have it. I want my family to have the life they deserve." Caroline feels her tears threatening. She blinks them away. She cannot fall apart. Not here. Not now. "Isaac loves you," she says, her voice cracking. "Give him a good life. Make him happy."

Flora's fingers tighten around the pouch of money. "And what of your children?"

At the thought of the children, Caroline's tears spill. "They can't know," she says. "They can't know any of it. And if I stay here, they will see who I truly am." It is suddenly hard to breathe.

Her children will be safe, she tells herself. Loved. They will have their father, their aunt. And they will know their mother as a good woman, not as a liar who seeks revenge. It is better this way. If she stays, they will be forced to watch as their father grows to hate their mother. They will be forced to hear of what she did to tear their family apart. They will grow up in a house full of bitterness and anger. Her children deserve better than that.

Pain seizes her throat. "You don't need to understand," she tells Flora. "You just need to do what I'm asking."

She turns away and pulls open the door. It must be now, before she changes her mind.

WILD

Down the stairs she goes, her eyes fixed on the door ahead. She cannot bear to think of anything else. Just that door. Just look. Just walk.

Caroline steps out into the street. She begins the long, steep trudge up the hill. None of this feels real.

Tonight she will tuck Gabriel into bed, will sing a lullaby to Mary, will fall asleep in Isaac's arms.

She needs to let herself believe this fantasy. If she thinks of how alone she will truly be tonight, she will not keep walking.

She hears footsteps behind her. No, she doesn't want footsteps. Does not want to be followed. Is it Flora with the money in her hands, pretending she wants her to stay? Or has Isaac seen her leave? Is he following her out of duty? She can't bear for it to be either of them.

"You're leaving?"

Caroline turns. She had not been expecting Scarlett. And she had not been expecting this bitterness in her voice. The sound of it makes Caroline's blood cold.

"Is it because of this?" Scarlett has a knife in one hand. A crumpled page in the other.

It takes a moment for Caroline to realise what it is. But when she does, her chest lurches.

'Jacob has left Talland.'

There is her carefully formed handwriting, crafted to look like someone else's. A record of all the dreadful things she has done. How long has Scarlett had this letter in her pocket? How long has she known?

"This is your handwriting," she says finally.

Caroline's throat tightens. "You can't be out here. Reuben's men may see you."

Scarlett shakes the letter at her. "What did you do?"

Caroline doesn't speak.

"Tell me!" cries Scarlett.

Yes, Caroline thinks, she owes her this. Owes her the truth. And so she meets Scarlett's eyes and says: "I forced your father to leave Talland." Her voice wavers, but she forces herself to continue. "I had Edward Baker show me who your mother was. He told me of how she brought you back across the cliffs on your way home from school. I told Jacob we were watching you. Said he was to leave the village. I told him his crew would kill you and your mother if he dared come back." She swallows heavily. "I told him he was to take the dory out and let the village believe he had drowned." The words are bitter on her lips. But she needs to keep speaking. Needs to tell Scarlett everything. Perhaps doing so will purge this poison from her body. Or perhaps she is just afraid of the silence that will follow. "Edward Baker followed him out to sea. Forced Jacob to tell him where he was going. We wanted to know he would do us no harm. Wanted to know he was truly gone."

Scarlett doesn't speak. Not for a long time. She just stands outside the inn with the knife in one hand and the letter in the other, the wind blowing her hair across furious eyes.

She is scared of her, Caroline realises. She has seen the intensity of the anger inside Scarlett. Knows there is no certainty that she will not die for this.

She longs to turn away. Look down. Look at the sea. Look anywhere but at Scarlett. But to do such a thing feels wrong. Feels as though she is shying away from all she has done. She holds Scarlett's gaze. Waits for the eruption. Perhaps, she waits to die.

"Why?" Scarlett asks finally.

"I thought I was doing it for love. I just did as he asked. I was a fool."

"He," Scarlett repeats. "Asher Hales."

Caroline nods.

Scarlett scrunches up the letter and shoves it back in her cloak pocket. "And now you are to walk away? Leave your children, just as you forced him to do?"

Caroline swallows the violent pain in her throat. "You know I have no choice."

"You're right," says Scarlett. "You don't."

Tears escape down Caroline's cheeks and she pushes them away. "They'll need you," she says. "Gabriel and Mary. And Isaac."

There is only silence.

"I'm so sorry, Scarlett," Caroline says finally. "More than you could know."

Still, Scarlett says nothing. Her dark eyes are unflinching, her knuckles white around the handle of the knife.

"Isaac cannot know any of this," Caroline coughs. "It will

kill him. You know it will." She meets Scarlett's eyes pleadingly. "If you love your brother, you will keep this to yourself. Please. I'm begging you." She knows she has no right to ask. But she does it anyway. She needs to believe that when she leaves this place, she will take the worst of her secrets with her.

Scarlett turns. Lets herself back into the inn without another word.

Scarlett goes to the cellar. From the top of the staircase, she looks down on Asher Hales. He is slumped against the top step, his wrists and ankles bound in mooring rope.

A prisoner. He deserves no better.

Scarlett realises she has the knife in her hand. She had not had any thought of it. Had she been holding it the whole time, she wonders? Had she been standing in the parlour watching the children play jacks, with a knife in her hand and blood on her boots? Had she been holding the knife to her chest like this as she had listened to Caroline's confession?

How many times had she stared at that letter and not seen the truth of who had written it? How many times had she been fooled by Caroline's carefully disguised hand? But this morning she had seen with fresh eyes.

Shock? Perhaps not as much as she ought to have felt. Because there had been Asher Hales outside their house. Caroline had been guarding secrets.

Guarding *this* secret.

Scarlett lights the lamp and pulls the cellar door closed behind her. Asher watches.

So it is like this. Her father had left his family on account of this man. Her mother had died of grief as a result of the things he had set in motion. He is a plotter. Manipulator. A man who uses his silky voice and handsome face to have others do his work. Strange, Scarlett thinks distantly, that a man with such talents might end up a prisoner.

She had been foolish enough to fall for him. But she sees now that she had not been the only one to do so.

She imagines Caroline hunched over her writing desk, scrawling this letter to the man she had loved. Thinks of the anger in her eyes when Asher had first arrived at their cottage. It hadn't been a look of anger at all, Scarlett realises. It had been a look of fear.

The man from the wreck had carried Caroline's darkest secrets ashore.

Scarlett kneels slowly beside Asher. He glances down at the knife, then looks up at her with shadowed eyes.

Before she knows what she is doing, Scarlett has the blade against his throat. "You forced my father to leave us."

"What are you talking about?" His voice is defiant, but something is passing across his face. Something that makes his jaw move and his eyes lose focus. Fear.

This coward.

"Don't lie to me," Scarlett hisses. "I saved your life."

"And now you will kill me?"

She stares at him. What would it be like, she wonders, to push that blade into his throat?

"Do it then," Asher says tiredly. "I'd expect no less from Jacob's daughter." His voice is hollow and empty. He is a man who has given up. A man with nothing to live for.

It would be easy. Draw the knife across his throat. Drag the body out through the tunnel and toss it into the sea. Cold and calculated, just like Jacob's murder of Reuben.

So be it. Asher Hales cannot be let free. One of them will have to kill him. And who better than her? She already has the darkness in her. Sooner or later, it will see her with blood on hands. Why fight it?

"Tell me the truth," she says. "Admit what you did."

She presses the blade into his throat. A tiny seam of blood appears on his pale skin.

"All right," he hisses. "Yes. I wanted Jacob gone. He deserved to be punished after framing me for murder."

Scarlett grits her teeth until pain shoots through her jaw.

"Do you wish you had let me die on that wreck?" Asher asks. "Do you wish I had let you go on believing a lie?"

She squeezes her eyes closed. A part of her longs for it more than anything. Longs for her heroic, dead father who had never killed a man. Longs for Caroline to be nothing more than the woman her brother had met at the tavern. The lies are much easier to carry than this betrayal.

She watches a thin trail of blood run onto the collar of Asher's shirt.

Her mind is cluttered. The only thought she can make sense of is this:

Asher Hales deserves to be punished. He deserves to die.

He deserves to have her push that blade deeper into his skin. Deeper and deeper until the blood runs out of him and he is sitting upright no more. The thought makes Scarlett hot with anticipation.

How right she was to send Jamie away.

There are footsteps. Someone is coming through the tunnel.

Out of the corner of her eye, Scarlett sees her father. Her father who had been forced to leave his family by Caroline and Asher Hales.

Why is he here? She can't make sense of it. He had killed Charles Reuben. He ought to be running.

She looks at Jacob, not removing the knife from Asher's throat. Ought she see him differently with this new information? Those tears she remembers from the night he had left had been the tears of a man forced from his home.

But when she looks at her father, all she sees is him driving his knife into Reuben's throat. The sight of it had sickened her. And here she is about to do the very same thing.

No. She will not kill Asher Hales. The thought is clearer than any others she has managed today.

She will not be like Jacob. She will not let the Wild win.

She inhales. And she is in control, she realises. With the clarity of her thoughts, the darkness inside her has loosened its grip.

She lowers the knife. Sets it on the floor.

And she sees that her father has not come through the tunnel alone.

There is Tom Leach, carrying a pistol, carrying a pick. His skin is dark and grimy, his beard a ragged mess.

Scarlett has never feared him before. But she sees now just what he is capable of. The man had blinded her, kidnapped the children, all for his own retribution. He has a gun in his hand, and no morals.

Scarlett eyes the knife she has placed on the floor.

"Don't," says Leach.

She looks questioningly at Jacob. Why are they together?

"I'm sorry, Scarlett," he says. "I came back to Talland to find you. I wanted to help you get away. But he found me outside your cottage. Said he knew I could find the money. He forced me to show him where it was hidden."

Scarlett's thoughts knock together. So Jacob had known the hiding place of the haul, just as Asher Hales had believed. How had Leach come to know of the money? How had he known who Jacob was? Seeing the man outside their cottage, she supposes, would have made it easy to guess. There is plenty of her in her father. Plenty of Isaac too.

Jacob had come back for them. Even with Reuben's blood staining his hands. He had come to help them get away. Scarlett knows Isaac had gone after their father that morning. Had something passed between them to make Jacob return?

She steps backwards towards the stairs. Leach trains his pistol on her. She clenches her teeth and fixes him with hard eyes.

"Untie me," says Asher. "I don't know how many people are upstairs. And if you leave me here, you'll be fighting them alone."

Leach runs his hand over the hole in the wall.

"It's not there," says Asher. "Any fool can see that." He glares at Jacob. "The man is lying to you. He's been lying to all of us."

Leach raps his knuckles against the rock. "Perhaps whoever went looking did not dig far enough." Finally, he makes his way across the cellar and unties the ropes binding Asher's wrists and ankles.

Asher stands slowly, rubbing the raw skin on his arms. He takes the knife from the floor and, with a smile on the edge of his lips, presses it hard to Scarlett's throat.

BLACK MAGIC

Flora turns away from the window. She does not want to see Caroline as she trudges up the hill.

She ought to go after her, she knows. Ought to send Isaac after her. But something stops her. Is it the knowledge that Caroline does not want to be followed? Perhaps.

Perhaps it is something else.

Flora sits with her back against the wall, her skirts pooling around her. She feels the weight of the silver in her pocket. Feels the solidity of this thing she had for so many years believed a myth.

She cannot take the money, of course. Cannot leave this place as Caroline had asked. The inn is her life. She will give the money to Isaac. But she can do no more. The Mariner's Arms has been in her family for generations. She will not see it turn to dust on her watch.

This place is home. Never mind the black magic in the

guestroom and the creaks in the night. This place is home.

The door opens. Isaac frowns at the sight of her on the floor. "Has something happened?"

She reaches into her pocket. Dumps the pouch of silver on the floor. A coin spills out and rolls across the room.

Isaac stares. "Where did this—"

"Caroline wants you to have it."

His lips part, but he doesn't speak. Perhaps finding an answer to this is far too difficult. He stares out the window. He must see her, surely, climbing the hill, disappearing from their lives. What is he thinking?

Flora pulls her knees to her chest. "You ought to go after her," she says finally.

"She found it in the cellar," says Isaac. It is not a question.

"I found the money," Flora admits. "By accident. It was hidden beneath the floor of the guestroom. I gave it to Caroline. She was to give it to Leach in exchange for Mary's life."

Isaac stares out the window. "You found it," he says, "but she was looking for it. Someone told her she would find it here. My father."

"Your father?"

Isaac says nothing.

"Whoever told her was wrong," Flora says finally. "Perhaps it was once in the cellar, but my father must have seen fit to move it. I don't know why."

Isaac turns away from the window. He sits beside her, his shoulder pressing against hers. "When I was a boy, I used to get out of bed in the night and watch the landing party come up the road. Carry their ankers into the inn. It stopped after your father died. After that, Jacob used the cave in Polperro to hide the goods."

Flora lets out her breath. "I knew nothing of it." What had gone on beneath her as a child, as she had slept upstairs in the inn? Were the creaks and thuds in her nightmares the footsteps of smugglers? "You think that's why my father moved the money upstairs? Because he was afraid the revenue men might search the cellar for contraband?"

"It's possible."

It is possible, of course. No doubt smugglers have been hiding their goods in the Mariner's Arms for as long as it has stood on this hill. The Mariner's Arms, Flora is coming to realise, is a place that knows how to keep secrets.

And the realisation comes. "The hole in the cellar wall. If it was dug by my father..." She inhales sharply. "If it was there when you and Jack were building the tunnel..." She fades out, unable to voice the words.

Isaac nods. "Ayes. It would have weakened the rock. It could have caused the tunnel to collapse."

Flora closes her eyes. She feels suddenly ill. And for a strange, drawn-out second, it feels as though the building is shifting around her. Feels as though all the death and darkness the place has seen is seeping from the walls.

Isaac presses a hand over hers. She wants to lace her fingers through his, wants to pull him closer. Wants him as a barrier between the inn and herself. But he pulls away too quickly. Climbs to his feet. "I need to go after her."

And Flora says: "Of course."

His footsteps are rhythmic as he makes his way towards the front door of the inn.

He does not know what he will say to her. Does not even know where to begin. He only knows that going after his wife is a duty. He cannot let her walk away.

Perhaps there is a part of him that wants to do so. But how will he look his children in the eye and tell them he let their mother leave?

He hears voices in the cellar. Men. And the sudden crack of pick against rock. The sound resonates through his body.

He slides his hand into the pocket of his coat, feels the cold metal of his pistol. He glances at the front door. Glances at the cellar. And he walks towards the thumping, the splintering, the men hiding beneath the inn.

He opens the cellar door a crack. And there is Tom Leach, heaving a pick into the wall. He is carving deep into the rock beneath, straying into the edge of the tunnel. Dirt rains over him, darkening his bare forearms and cheeks. And there is Scarlett, there is their father. Jacob is standing with his back pressed to the wall, arms folded across his chest. What is he doing here? Is he working with Leach? Isaac knows he cannot put it past him.

Asher stands with an arm clamped around Scarlett's front, a knife held to her neck. Isaac sees her eyes dart to him. She looks away hurriedly.

His hand tightens around his pistol. How long will it be before Leach realises the money is no longer in the wall?

He curses silently. He has been foolish. Had assumed Leach neither brave nor foolish enough to return to Talland while the revenue men are prowling. And he had been naïve enough to believe Flora when she'd assured him Leach was too afraid to enter the Mariner's Arms.

He wants to shoot. Desperately, urgently wants to shoot. Damn the consequences or the guilt. He just wants to see

Leach dead. But he is outnumbered. Act rashly and Asher will have that knife in Scarlett's throat.

"Dead men walk that tunnel," Scarlett tells Leach. "Perhaps you'll disturb them." She is infuriatingly brazen. Isaac wills her to stay quiet.

Leach looks over his shoulder to glare at her. His eyes glow in the dusty pits of his cheeks.

"I told you," says Asher. "I told you it's not there."

Leach hurls the pick across the cellar. It clatters into a pile of broken chairs and sends shards of wood flying. He marches up to Scarlett. "Where is it?"

She gives him steely eyes, Asher's knife still hard against her throat. "Why are you asking me?"

Isaac watches his father move silently across the cellar. Behind Leach's back. Out of Asher's eyeline. He disappears into the tunnel.

Scarlett's gaze doesn't falter. "It's a myth," she tells Leach.

"It's no myth. Your brother's wife, she knew of it. Knew how to get to it."

Isaac feels a tug in his chest. He forces himself to focus.

"My brother's wife has left," says Scarlett. "Perhaps she's taken the money with her."

Leach pulls his pistol.

Isaac lifts his gun higher. He tries to align the barrel with Leach's head. Here at the top of the stairs, the angle is wrong. He will need to step down into the cellar. He holds his breath and pushes on the door. The hinges creak noisily.

He hears Leach's shot, feels the burn above his elbow. And somehow Scarlett is at his side, gripping his shoulder, calling his name.

She runs a hand over the worn timber of the door frame.

The wood has splintered where the bullet has lodged inside. "The bullet is in the wall," she says. "It's just grazed you."

The pain is disorienting, and she sounds far away. The bullet is in the wall, he tells himself. It does little to help the burn, but it does slow the racing of his heart. He grips his arm, watching beads of blood drizzle out between his fingers.

Flora is waiting in the tavern. Ready. The gunshot rattles her. She runs down into the cellar. Lets out her breath at the sight of the blood staining the arm of Isaac's shirt. She looks past him at Asher and Leach.

She is ready, she reminds herself. Caroline had warned her these men would come.

"You want the money," she says, standing at the top of the cellar stairs and looking down at them. The lantern in her hand makes shadows on their faces. She steps back as they approach. The two men climb the stairs, their pistol and knife keeping Isaac and Scarlett at bay.

Leach shoves his way to the front. Behind him, Asher Hales waits, watches.

Leach's eyes dart as he steps into the bar. Flora has made it a frightening place, just for him. The watch ball hanging above the stairs, the bottle of dried blood on the counter. In the dim light, it is easy to believe the Mariner's Arms is a place of ghosts and demons and all those things her mother had feared. Leach is afraid of this place, Flora knows. Perhaps she is a little afraid of this place too.

"Do you have it, witch?" he hisses.

Flora nods.

237

His eyes flash. She knows he wants to come after her. Wants to strike her, knock her down. But what might such a thing cause? He believes her capable of calling the devil and sending ships to the ocean floor. Think of what she could do to a mortal like him.

She climbs the stairs. Can hear their footsteps behind her, heavy and rhythmic.

Leach turns his pistol to Asher, warning him to stay back. And Asher stays, because he is a coward.

Flora leads Leach past her mother's room, past Jack's room, into the third guestroom. Shards of the black mirror crunch beneath her boots.

Leach steps inside uncertainly. She sees his eyes move over the half-planed letters carved into the wall, over the filthy rug, over the loose floorboard that had hidden the silver.

There is a great power to this, Flora realises. A great power to this craft her mother had made her life. Is it magic? Perhaps. After all, the healing water had brought back Scarlett's sight. Perhaps it is magic, but perhaps it is more about manipulation. Perhaps the power lies in taking a man's fear and making him believe.

She will not lose sight of her rationality, her reason. But she cannot discount the craft entirely. Because her mother's black mirror, Flora has come to realise, is far more than just a parlour trick. She has seen men's deaths in that dark glass. And she has seen fire rip through her inn, burning it to the ground.

"Where is the money?" Leach demands. He holds the gun out in front of him. Flora knows it is empty. He had fired at Isaac. Had not had time to reload.

She nods towards the loose floorboards. "Under there."

Leach eyes her hesitantly. He goes to the corner of the

room. Prises up the boards.

And there is nothing, of course. The silver is heavy in Flora's pocket.

Her heart is thumping. How will all this happen, she wonders? The details in the glass have been unclear. But she is suddenly, deathly certain that tomorrow, she will not be reopening the Mariner's Arms.

She pulls aside the rug. Sets the lantern on the floor, its flame lighting the indents of the circle.

Leach looks back at her. With the light beneath him, his face is strangely shadowed. He looks old and worn. "Where is the money, witch?" he demands. And then he looks down. Looks down at the rough-hewn circle with which Flora's mother had sought to change the images in the glass. The circle she had believed was full of dark magic. The circle she believed had unleashed demons into her home.

Leach stares at his boots. They have inched across the outer edge of the ring. "What is this?" The malice in his voice has given way to terror.

And Flora has no thought of where her answer comes from. The words escape on their own accord. "A man who steps inside the circle," she says calmly, "is a man destined to die."

She sees the flame come at her as Leach grabs the lantern and hurls it in horror. The lamp flies past her and splinters against the window.

Leach rushes from the room.

And Flora turns to watch the flames climbing their way up the curtains. They tear through the dry, dusty fabric and race towards the thick beams of the roof. She feels the smoke in her throat, in her eyes. But the sight of it is mesmerising. She cannot look away.

She glances down at the circle. Black magic? Or just a trick of the mind? Either way, it had been a frighteningly easy line to cross.

She feels a firm hand around her arm. She turns, expecting Isaac. But Asher Hales is standing close, his breath hot and stale against her cheek. He seems to barely notice the fire.

"The money," he hisses. "Where is it?"

Flora digs into her pocket and pulls out the coin pouch.

Asher stares. "No. That cannot be all of it."

She looks him squarely in the eye. "This is all of it. It's just one man's share."

His lip curls. "Give it to me."

This money is not intended for men like Asher Hales. This money is intended for Isaac to build his new life. But Asher has Scarlett's knife in his hand. Smoke is pushing into the passage and flames are climbing the rafters. Soon this place will crumble.

Flora hears Isaac calling her name. They need to leave. Need to get their children out safely. She cannot stay and fight Asher Hales.

And so she upends the bag of silver into the room, kicking the coins in the direction of the flames. Asher shoves her away and darts towards them, dropping desperately onto his hands and knees.

Isaac grabs Flora's arm and pulls her from the burning room. A cloth is knotted around his upper arm, an ink stain of blood darkening the fabric. "Quickly," he says. "We need to leave."

Bessie darts out of the parlour and runs towards Jack's room. Flames are beginning to lick the doorframe. Flora snatches her arm, yanking her back as a wall of heat slams them.

Is this, she wonders fleetingly, what her mother had sought

to reverse? Had she seen a snowy-haired girl in her mirror, dashing through the burning rooms of the Mariner's Arms? She will never know, of course, not for certain. But today she has begun to understand the allure of black magic.

"Downstairs," Flora tells her daughter sharply. "Quickly."

Bessie grips her dog, her eyes full of tears. "What about all the flowers?"

Yes, the flowers will burn in their pouches and pockets. They will burn along with her mother's chest. The lambswool will bubble and the polished shelves will splinter away. The fire will take the room in which she had been born, in which she had stitched her wedding dress, become a mother.

It will take the floorboards that had hidden the silver. Take the cellar stairs worn thin by smugglers' boots. It will blacken the tunnel in which Jack had died.

Tomorrow, this place will be a cold stone shell. The rain and the wind will beat it down until there is nothing left.

Flora cannot bring herself to feel sorrow. Cannot bring herself to feel anger. Because she knows, somewhere deep inside, that Tom Leach has brought her exactly what she had wanted.

Leave through the front door and Reuben's men will find them. They must go through the tunnel and wait on the beach for dark. Wait for Will Francis to appear in that boat that will take them away from Talland.

Isaac opens the cellar door, letting smoke billow in from the bar. He slams it hurriedly behind them.

Dust is raining down over the tunnel opening, the wall to

one side a gaping mess. Bricks and earth are strewn over the floor, along with Leach's discarded pick.

Step carefully.

Isaac takes the lamp from above the stairs. He hands it to Flora for lighting. She shines the lantern into the tunnel and clutches her daughter's hand. And in they go, Flora and Bessie first, Scarlett with Mary in her arms. Isaac hunches and steps into the passage, a hand pressed to Gabriel's shoulder.

Something is not right. He hears that groan of shoring timber, that strange raspy breath of the rock. Sounds he has heard so many times in his sleep.

He grabs a fistful of Gabriel's coat and throws him back towards the cellar. He hollers for Scarlett, for Flora.

They have heard it too; that groan above their heads. Have felt the trickle of stone against their cheeks. There is no time for thinking, only for running.

The rock roars as it falls. Earth spills from above as the hacked-at shoring timbers splinter beneath the weight. And it is all sickeningly familiar as Isaac scrambles forward, breathless, and lands hard on his hands and knees on the floor of the cellar. Pain shoots through his arm. He clambers away from the opening, shielding his son. There is dust and smoke and rock and noise.

And then it is over. As sudden and incomprehensible as it had been the first time.

For a second he is afraid to open his eyes. He hears Mary shriek wildly. Feels Gabriel crawl out from beneath him. And he looks.

There is Gabriel and Mary and Scarlett. But there is no one else.

Scarlett clamps a hand over her mouth to stop a violent sob.

For a moment, Isaac is frozen, staring into the black pile of debris where the tunnel had once been.

None of this is real, of course. How can it be? It is too quick, too sudden, too brutal. In a moment the cellar door will open and Flora will find him, her daughter hovering at her side. He feels himself grapple at the image of it, trying desperately to make it real.

He calls her name. And there is nothing. Just Mary whining into Scarlett's shoulder and a distant crash from the inn above their heads.

Scarlett's voice is hushed and broken as she says: "We need to leave."

THE ESCAPING SOUL

Flames are curling around the bannister, pushing their way into the bar.

"The door at the back is blocked," Scarlett says breathlessly. "We need to go out through the front."

Isaac tries to focus. Tries to push aside the violent pain in his chest. He cannot think. Not now. He has to get his family to safety.

There will be men waiting outside, he is sure, waiting to punish them for Reuben's murder. Men that will have been alerted to their presence by the smoke streaming from the Mariner's Arms. But they have no choice but to go this way.

Villagers have gathered at the edge of the road, watching, murmuring. Martha Francis is hurrying towards them. Isaac cannot look at her. Cannot bear to answer her questions. Cannot bring himself to put to words all that has happened. If he speaks of it he will crumble.

He sees Ned Arthur on the other side of the road. "The banker," says Isaac. "Have you seen him?"

Arthur's eyes are on the flames pouring out the upstairs windows. "Saw him on the beach. You think he's there waiting for you?"

Isaac glances past him. If the banker is waiting on the beach, there will no doubt be more of Reuben's men prowling Bridles Lane. They will not have their escape easily.

He looks up at the church spire cutting through the trees. "The bell house," he says, catching Scarlett's eye.

Where else is there to go?

Asher Hales hurries down the staircase, landing heavily on his knees on the floor of the tavern. His lungs are burning and water streams from his eyes. His shirt is damp with sweat. But none of that matters. Because Henry Avery's haul is in his pocket.

He hears a crowd outside the door. He cannot go this way. No one can see him. What if they are somehow able to see the treasure he is carrying? Too many people know of this money. Too many greedy, untrustworthy people.

He snatches a poker from beside the fireplace and smashes one of the narrow windows at the side of the inn. He scrambles out of it, falling to his knees and coughing the smoke from his lungs. After a few moments, he stands dizzily, drawing down long breaths of air. He begins to walk.

For a few yards, he follows the stream carved into the hill behind the inn. And when he is sure he is alone, he pulls the pouch from his pocket. Stares into it. He shifts the bag from one hand to the other. It is real. It is here. It is his.

He smiles a real smile. When was the last time he had done such a thing?

There are other things in the pouch too. Shards of black glass he had scooped from the floor in his desperation to reach the silver. He lifts one out and turns it over in his hand. Then he tosses it into the stream, letting the water carry it towards the sea. He hears a distant roar as the Mariner's Arms spills its insides.

And he begins to walk. Up the hill he will go, away from Talland, away from Cornwall. East, then east and east again, until he reaches London.

He is beginning to remember himself. Beginning to remember who Asher Hales was always supposed to be. A pioneer. A man of science. A man who is better than the rest.

Tom Leach stands ahead of him on the path. Asher can't help but laugh. Poor, foolish Tom Leach who had turned away from a fortune because of a woman's trickery.

There is a gun in his hand.

Asher glances at it. He knows he ought to be afraid. He is always afraid. But somehow, this new-found wealth has given him courage. He takes Scarlett's knife from his pocket.

"Why have you come looking for trouble?" he asks Leach. "Don't you know you're going to die? You stepped inside the witch's circle." The words are so foolish he almost laughs, but he sees the terror in Leach's eyes.

"The money. Give it to me." Leach raises his pistol. There is a tremor in his hand. He has a gun and Asher only a knife, but it is Leach who is afraid.

Can a man bring about his own death, Asher finds himself wondering? Can the mind convince the body to die? A fascinating concept.

Leach's shot is wild with terror. It flies over Asher's shoulder. And before he can think of what he is doing, Asher has his knife in Leach's throat. Wine-dark blood fountains over his fingers.

What a feeling of power.

Leach falls across the thick muck of the path, animalistic rasps coming from his throat. And Asher's heart begins to speed. This is the moment he has been chasing his entire adult life. The moment of death. The escape of the soul.

He almost laughs. For years he has been trying to witness this moment. And in the end, all he needed was to kill a man himself. How simple. How achingly perfect.

He watches. Leans close to the body. He cannot miss a thing.

Look; twitching of the arms and legs. The departing soul causing movement as it escapes. Watch as the eyes turn to glass; a sign that the body is now no more than a shell. He looks upwards. Can the soul be seen?

There, above the body. A shifting of the air. So subtle it is almost imperceptible. But Asher is certain. The soul escaping. If they were in darkness, he is certain, the escaping life force would shine like the corpse lights as it moves away from the body. Perhaps such a thing could be measured. Recorded. Extensively researched.

For a long time, Asher sits beside Leach's still form.

He will go to London and present these ideas in the coffee houses. Share them among his fellow students, his fellow surgeons, his fellow inquiring minds.

He takes the pistol from Leach's motionless hand. Reaches into his coat pocket for the powder flask and balls. He opens the chamber and pours the powder in carefully.

Soon, Asher Hales will be a great man. And Caroline Bailey will realise it. She will crawl from the wreckage of her life and come to him. This money in his pocket will see him to greatness. Fame. It will be easy for Caroline to find him. Because he will be the man who shines like the brightest of stars.

The church is empty but for a woman praying close to the altar. Sunlight spears the coloured window, but does little to light the nave. The smell of smoke hangs in the air, clinging to their clothing, their hair, the sky.

Scarlett goes to the window and tries to peer through. Tries to catch a glimpse of the banker.

He had been waiting for her and Isaac on the beach, back when she was a child. Fourteen years later, he is still waiting. There has to be an end to it.

Isaac follows her into the churchyard. They peer down at the beach. There he is, the tiny figure of the banker, pacing the sand, watching, waiting.

"Stay low," Isaac hisses, pushing her to the ground. "Don't let him see you."

Scarlett lies on her front at the edge of the rock face, feeling the wind rush up to meet her.

The banker will find them if they take the cliff path. Will find them if they try and leave by sea, now the eastern beach is inaccessible. He will surely have stationed men at the top of Bridles Lane.

Why such loyalty to Reuben, Scarlett wonders? Even after his death?

She sucks in her breath. There is a boat on the edge of the bay, moving steadily towards them. She squints. Her vision feels cloudy, unreliable. "Can you see who it is?"

"Ayes," says Isaac. "It's Jacob."

They watch in silence. Watch him slide through the water towards them, slowly, silently, behind the eyes of the banker. Watch him come to help them escape, as he had returned to Talland to do.

Isaac looks over the edge of the cliff. "We've got to climb down."

Scarlett's eyes follow his. The rock is rugged and dark. Vertical, no. But not far from it. Waves beat relentlessly up against the base.

"It's climbable," says Isaac.

She wants to believe him. Wants to believe they have a means of escape. But the rocks are slippery with sea mist and rain. She knows, beneath his coat, the sleeve of Isaac's shirt is darkening with blood.

"You've been hurt," she says. "How can you climb?"

He squeezes her shoulder, and climbs to his feet. "We've no choice."

Scarlett searches the church. There is no rope. Nothing that will help them scale the rock. But they are hidden in a curve of the cliff. From here the banker will not see them.

And so, they will climb.

Isaac and Scarlett take the children out to the graveyard. They pass the headstones of their family, pass their father's memorial. They pass the grave of Martha's mother behind which the signalling lanterns hide.

Scarlett takes Mary from Isaac. The bullet is in the wall, she reminds herself, with flames on all sides. Still, he cannot climb the cliffs with a child beneath his arm.

"Let me take her down," she says.

Isaac unwinds the scarf from around his neck. He ties it tightly around Scarlett's front, latching Mary to her back.

Scarlett tucks up her skirts. They have to go. Now. Before Reuben's men see Jacob in the bay. She peers over the edge at the sea thrashing the headland. Mary's legs curl around her waist.

And they climb because they have no choice. Rock slides beneath their boots, sending earth raining into the sea. Scarlett's knuckles whiten as she grips the slippery crag. One step, she tells herself. Then another, another. Like walking the clifftop in the dark. To the side of her, Isaac and Gabriel are climbing slowly, steadily. She sees them speak to each other, their words lost beneath the roar of the sea.

Scarlett's boots touch the rocks at the base of the cliff. A swell of sea rolls towards her, tugging at her ankles, trying to pull her off balance. She dares to glance over her shoulder. Jacob is close. His boat is bumping and grinding against the rock. The water is too shallow for him to come any closer.

Scarlett times her run across the rocks with the inhalation of the sea. Mary wriggles and bleats, trying to escape the confines of the tightly knotted scarf.

Jacob reaches out a hand and helps her into the boat.

With five people aboard, the dory sits low in the water, the swell pushing over the gunwale. They keep close to the cliffs, away from the eyes of the banker.

Isaac takes off his coat and snatches an oar from his father. He begins to row.

"You've been hurt," says Jacob.

Isaac shakes his head dismissively, though Scarlett can see beads of sweat glistening on his forehead. The dory tilts on the swell. They pull away from the cliff, towards the open water.

Jacob looks at Scarlett. He nods towards the pocket of his coat. "In there."

She reaches inside. Finds a large key.

"My cottage in Portreath," says Jacob. "You'll be safe there."

"What about you?"

"I've no one after me," he says. "The two of you will need it more."

Is she to say *come with us*? Is she to invite him back into their lives? She can't bring herself to do it. Even after all she has learnt, Jacob Bailey is still the man with blood on his hands. He is everything she does not want to become.

She doesn't speak. Just nods silently and slips the key into her pocket.

Asher stands at the edge of the cliff.

He looks at the pistol. Looks down at the boat.

He has one shot.

Who is this bullet for? Scarlett Bailey, who had drawn his blood? Isaac, who had taken the woman he loves and made her his wife?

No, each would be a waste.

What a potent thing it is to be a man strong enough to take a life. He feels dizzy with the power of it. And this power ought not be wasted.

This bullet is for one man and one man alone.

SILENCE

He is alive. And then he is gone.

The shot comes from the clifftops. Finds Jacob's chest. There is barely a sound, and not a hint of warning. Jacob's body falls backwards, the oar sliding from his hands. His death is sudden and still and silent.

Scarlett holds her breath. She waits for the next gunshot. Waits to die. But there is only quiet. Only the water lapping at the side of the boat.

And so Jacob Bailey is dead. Scarlett has gotten what she had wished for in the darkest, most bitter moments of the Wild.

She looks down at her father's face. He is expressionless, blank, the breeze moving the unruly grey thatch of his hair. She reaches over and closes his eyes.

She looks at her brother. His eyes are fixed to the bloom of blood spreading across Jacob's chest. Scarlett looks up at the clifftop. There is no one there. Whoever had pulled the trigger is gone.

Isaac clears his throat. "Help me." His voice is husky.

Scarlett nods. They will send Jacob's body to the sea floor, back to the place it has always been.

She pulls Mary around to her front. Unties the scarf and hands the baby to Gabriel. The children watch with wide, silent eyes.

Scarlett reaches an arm beneath her father's body. She feels the weight of him, feels his fading warmth. She and Isaac lift him over the gunwale. And down his body goes into the waiting sea.

Scarlett feels an unbidden swell of emotion. She covers her mouth, forcing her sob back inside. It doesn't feel right to break this stillness. Tears blur her vision. Are they tears for Flora and Bessie, or tears for her father? She blinks them away hurriedly. She cannot allow herself to crumble. Not here. Not now. Not until they are safe.

She presses a hand to her chest as a striking, physical pain wells up inside her. She leans over the gunwale and watches the last shadow of her father disappear. "He didn't want to leave us," she says. "He was forced to."

Isaac turns to look at her. "By who?" There is a thinness to his voice and she can tell he is afraid of the answer.

Scarlett reaches into her pocket for the letter. She screws it into her fist. Slips it over the edge to follow Jacob's body to the sea floor. "Asher Hales."

She shuffles onto the bench and takes up the seat left empty by her father. Begins to pull the oar through the water. The patch of sea beneath which Jacob lies becomes lost in the enormity of the ocean.

"The eastern beach." Isaac's voice is caught in his throat. "We need to check."

Scarlett nods wordlessly. She presses a hand over her brother's and squeezes tightly.

They row in silence, the oars sighing through the sea. Scarlett is desperate to make it around the headland, desperate to leave Talland and the banker and the invisible shooter behind. Desperate to leave Jacob's circle of sea and the funnel of smoke above the Mariner's Arms.

But she cannot bear to look as they round the point to the eastern beach. Cannot bear to have this tiny flicker of hope torn away.

She doesn't look over her shoulder. Can't manage even the briefest of glances at the beach beyond the tunnel.

Isaac leaps into the shallow water.

Still Scarlett can't look. Her heart is pounding.

"Flora and Bess," she says. "Are they there? Are they safe?"

Gabriel is on his feet, watching the beach, making the boat tilt and the baby squeal. And he is garbling, *ayes Aunt Scarlett, they are there, they are safe.*

She dares to turn. Sees Isaac in the water, thrashing towards the shore. Sees Flora and Bessie at the edge of the sand, the dark mouth of the tunnel behind them. The dog is running in circles around the narrow curve of the beach.

Scarlett hears a cry of relief escape her. The gratitude makes her body hot and tired and achy and alive; all these things at once. She watches Isaac take Flora in his arms. And Scarlett brings the boat closer, closer until the oars graze the bottom of the sea.

Flora lifts Bessie into the boat, then lets Isaac help her inside. And then they are rowing again, around the point, beneath the plume of smoke that is palling the village.

Isaac takes one hand from the oar. He slides his fingers through Flora's. And Scarlett can tell by the look in his eyes that he can't bring himself to let go.

TOMORROW

"Ground ivy," says Flora. "It will help it heal." She pins the strapping around Isaac's arm and carefully pulls down his shirtsleeve. Her fingers ghost over his skin.

He gives her a smile. "Thank you." Slightly rigid, slightly stilted. Things have shifted. Everything is different.

Flora holds his gaze for a moment, then sweeps the last scraps of ivy from the table and tosses them into the fire. She goes to the sleeping pallet in the corner of the room where Bessie is curled up on her side, the dog snoring at her feet.

Jacob's cottage is tiny, crowded with them all inside.

When they had arrived here, two days after escaping Talland, Isaac had found himself oddly drawn to the tin cups, the bowls, the candle holders lining the shelves. Had found himself peeking into the storage chest and feeling the coat, the mittens, the worn woollen cap that lay inside. He couldn't make sense of why. Was it grief for his father that had him rifling through his things? Curiosity? All he had learned about Jacob's disappearance had him questioning who the man had truly been.

He had found a stash of money in a jar beside the flour. No fortune, but enough for those elusive tickets out of Cornwall.

This is not the way he had imagined his escape. Caroline had always pushed so strongly for their freedom. It doesn't feel right to be doing this without her. But just how real, he wonders now, were any of the plans he and his wife had made? Just how real had any of their life been?

There is bitterness in his throat at the thought of all he has learned. And there are questions he feels sure he will never know the answers to. Questions he is not sure he wants answered.

He does not know what to think. Does not know what it is he is feeling. Is it grief, or anger or betrayal or sorrow? Perhaps it is all these things at once.

But he will keep moving. Tomorrow, they will take a coach to Penzance and find the ship that will carry them north, away from a life of free trade. Perhaps he is feeling grief and anger and betrayal and sorrow, but he is also feeling hope.

He tosses another log on the fire, sending sparks shooting up the chimney.

Gabriel is asleep by the hearth, curled up on his side with a hand splayed out in front of him. Isaac sits. Presses a hand to his son's shoulder, feeling his body rise and fall with breath.

On the other side of the room, he hears them murmuring, Flora and Bessie, whispering to each other in their hushed and musical way. He dares to glance across the room at them; their matching faces, their pressed-together knees, the cascades of silver-blonde hair.

There is a part of him, of course, that wants to go to her. That part of him that had longed for more when her fingers had grazed his forearm. That part of him that had been as excited as a child when she'd said, *yes Isaac, I will climb on that ship beside you.*

But everything is different. Strange. Dizzying. Being with Flora is no longer about escape, about vanishing fleetingly from the strain of the world around them. The moment he walks across the room and takes her in his arms, it will make this real.

Right now, there is the shadow of Caroline. There is their hazy, unformed future and there are answers to find to his son's impossible questions. He cannot allow himself to think of that warmth she leaves inside him. Cannot allow himself to think of how it feels to hold her in the dark.

So for now, he will just think of how calming it is to hear her breathe in the night. Will think of the heart-splitting gratitude he had felt when he had found her safe at the end of the tunnel. Will think of how glad he is that she will be there when he wakes.

In the morning, Scarlett walks with them into the village.

"You will write, ayes?" she asks. "The very moment you're settled?"

Isaac smiles. "The very moment."

She knots her fingers in her shawl. There is the carriage, on the edge of the village green. There is the coachman, heaving trunks onto the roof and tying them with rope. The sight of it makes this real.

"And the children?" she asks. "You'll manage?" There is guilt in her for leaving them. Leaving Isaac with only pieces of the truth. Guilt at leaving him to build a new life in the wake of the things he has learned. After all the years she has spent longing to be a help to her brother, is she truly to leave him now, when he needs her the most?

"You've to make your own life, Scarlett," he says firmly. "I'll not have you lose that chance because of me." He squeezes her shoulders. "Besides, we'll not be alone."

No, she thinks, a faint smile on her lips. They will not be alone. The thought of it leaves a warmth inside her.

She throws her arms around Isaac's neck, her throat tightening.

How is she to do this; live a life without her brother to anchor her? The thought of it is far too overwhelming. But she knows it is time to do so. She cannot stay latched to him forever.

She steps back, swiping at the tears she is unable to contain.

"Are you certain?" Isaac asks, his hand still around her wrist.

She nods. Her throat, her chest are aching, but yes. Certain. "I'll see you again, ayes?" she says, her voice wavering. "Promise me I'll see you again."

"Of course." Scarlett can tell he is trying for lightness, but she hears the emotion thickening his words. He kisses her cheek. "Of course you'll see us again. You'll see us again before you know it."

And so she watches as they climb aboard the coach that will take them to the harbour in Penzance. Watches as the carriage gets smaller and smaller until there is nothing but hills and sky.

She stands outside Jamie's cottage for a long time. She is a mess. She has no bonnet, no comb, no clean clothes. But she also has no weapon. She has no idea what has become of her knife. But she doesn't want it. Perhaps she doesn't need it. Perhaps she can be a person who is in control.

She wants to be someone without blood on her boots or a blade at her knee. And if she knocks on Jamie's door, she will have to keep this promise to herself and be just that.

Perhaps he will turn her away. Perhaps he has already seen too much. Perhaps she ought to have climbed into the carriage with Isaac and Flora.

She knocks. And there is nothing but silence. It does little to ease the thundering in her chest.

For a moment she thinks of leaving. Thinks to walk back up the hill to that lonely cottage where her father had spent so much of his life.

No. She does not want to be Jacob.

Rain begins to spill. It streams across the cobbles and turns the edges of the road to mud. Scarlett presses her back against Jamie's door. Water runs from the thin edge of the awnings and drizzles down her neck.

It is dusk when she sees him. He is in his neat blue uniform, hands dug into his pockets and a scarf bound tight at his neck. Water drips from the ends of his hair.

At the sight of her, he stops striding. Smiles.

"I'm glad you're happy to see me," she says throatily.

He pulls a key from his pocket and slides it into the lock. "I'm happy to see my lodgings. It's a good night to be inside." He chuckles at Scarlett's uncertain expression. Puts a hand to her shoulder to usher her into the house. "I'm happy to see you too. Very happy."

They stand opposite each other, letting pools of silver water gather at their feet. With Jamie's eyes on hers, Scarlett's carefully rehearsed words become a tangled mess.

"It's cold," she manages.

Jamie takes the tinderbox from the shelf and crouches to light the fire. When he looks back at her, one side of his face is lit with the glow of the gathering flames.

"My father is dead," she says.

He stands. "Scarlett, I'm sorry, I—"

"I'm not telling you for your sympathy. I'm telling you because…" She fades out. How does she put into words this new control she feels inside her? This belief that, on the day of her father's death, the Wild's hold on her had died too? How does she explain the way she had felt the anger release her when she had lowered that knife from Asher's throat?

The Wild is still there, of course. She knows it has not left her. It is in her blood, it never will. But she will not let it take her to the dark places it had taken her father. She will not let it put a dead man at her feet.

She says: "I was wrong to let you leave."

She feels painfully vulnerable. Knows there is every chance Jamie could shake his head and send her away.

He steps close and takes her hands. Runs a finger over the curve of her thumbnail. "I have nothing to give you," he says after a moment. "I don't even have an oven."

Scarlett smiles slightly. "What need do we have for an oven?"

His grip on her hands tightens. "I'm out until dawn several nights a week. And I'm terrible in the mornings."

She raises her eyebrows. "Are you trying to turn me away?"

"No." He presses a hand to her cheek. "No. I just want you to know what this life will be."

Yes, she sees a glimpse of this life. She sees herself walking through the village to distrustful whispers as the smugglers do their best to keep their secrets away from her ears. She sees herself battle to keep her anger inside. And she sees nights of lying alone in the dark, terrified that Jamie might entangle himself with men as ruthless as Tom Leach.

She sees this imperfect life and she wants it anyway.

She kneels by the edge of the hearth. Jamie sits beside her, his wet shoulder pressing against hers. Steam curls from their clothes, hot and white in the firelight.

"Does this mean you're staying?" he asks.

Scarlett smiles to herself. She has much to tell him. Tales of collapsing tunnels and burning inns. The stray bullet that had flown from the clifftops. There is Reuben's murder and the silver beneath the floor and the smugglers' banker pacing the beach. She wants to tell him it all. Every piece.

She holds her hands to the fire. Stares into the light.

By now, the ship will have left Penzance harbour, taking her brother northward towards islands and snow. By now, she is sure, the Mariner's Arms is nothing but a shell, and Charles Reuben is deep in the earth of their churchyard.

And just beyond, in the inky blue of the bay, a man lies on the floor of the sea. From the top of the cliff his memorial stone watches, having waited almost two decades for him to arrive.

HISTORICAL NOTE ON THE WEST COUNTRY TRILOGY

When Richard Dodge became the vicar of Talland Church in 1713, he quickly developed something of a reputation. Dodge became famous across the county as a ghost and demon hunter, known for his ability to cast restless souls away from the land of the living. He conducted regular exorcisms in Bridles Lane (also spelled Bridals Lane) and was sought out by everyone from parishioners to fellow clergymen when the supernatural ventured a little too near.

Dodge's most famous feat took place in 1725, when he was approached by Mr Gryllis, a rector in nearby Lanreath to lay the ghosts of headless horses several villagers had seen on the moors. Dodge supposedly caught sight of these ghostly horses, only to discover they pulled a carriage transporting the devil himself. Dodge proceeded to exorcise the moor, causing the spectral carriage to be pulled back to Hell. Records of this event exist in Talland Church's archives to this day.

Though we can surmise Dodge's exorcisms were a cover

for local smuggling activities— of which the vicar would have undoubtedly received a cut— his demon-filled sermons would have been readily believed by the superstitious population of eighteenth-century Talland.

Richard Dodge remained vicar of the parish until 1746, when he died at the age of ninety-three. His body is buried at the top end of the churchyard, close to where the cemetery gives way to the sea.

There are many theories surrounding the haul of Henry Avery, widely acknowledged as one of the most prosperous pirates in history. His looting of the treasure ship *Gunsway* in 1695 remains the biggest single pirate raid ever recorded, with the haul totalling approximately $100 million in today's currency.

One of the most enduring theories suggests Avery hid his wealth in the cliffs of south Cornwall. A letter supposedly written by Avery to a close friend detailed three chests of jewels and gold buried close to Lizard Point. So convincing was this piece of evidence that, in 1779, three men from Saint Michael's Mount embarked on a two-year treasure hunt, hacking into the cliffs at the south-west tip of the county. The hunt came to an end when one of Avery's descendants told the men his ancestor had died penniless in Barnstable, north Devon.

While there is no evidence to suggest any of Henry Avery's haul ever made its way to Talland, seventeenth century pirates' articles dictated that any takings be distributed fairly between the captain and ship's hands. As a result, numerous shares of the *Gunsway's* haul would no doubt have found their way back to England in the possession of Avery's crew.

All incantations and healing charms, from the bags of good luck Meg gives her visitors in *Moonshine (Prequel)* to the fire-warmed stones for the child's-cough (whooping cough) Flora uses in *Bridles Lane*, are based on ancient Cornish healing lore. The arrangement of letters on the wall of the guestroom in *Wild Light* is known at the Sator Square:

S A T O R
A R E P O
T E N E T
O P E R A
R O T A S

Utilised extensively throughout Cornwall as a charm against black magic, the square was also used as far back as the first century, having been discovered on ancient Roman drinking vessels and carved into columns in the buried ruins of Pompeii and Herculaneum. Its function in Roman times remains unclear.

To this day, practitioners of herbal lore and ancient Cornish witchcraft can be found around the county.

ABOUT THE AUTHOR

Johanna Craven is an Australian-born writer, pianist and film composer. She loves travelling, meditative dance and playing the folk fiddle. Johanna divides her time between London and Melbourne, escaping to Cornwall— one of her favourite places in the world— as often as she can.

Find out more at www.johannacraven.com.

Printed in Great Britain
by Amazon

37433866R00161